OTHER BOOKS BY THE AUTHOR

Short Ropes, long falls, prison walls;

Hungry inmates may become violent inmates;

Most uncommon events at Ryan Park.

COYOTE
AND
MAGPIE

DUANE SHILLINGER

authorHOUSE®

AuthorHouse™
1663 Liberty Drive
Bloomington, IN 47403
www.authorhouse.com
Phone: 1 (800) 839-8640

Published by AuthorHouse 08/20/2018

ISBN: 978-1-5462-5651-9 (sc)
ISBN: 978-1-5462-5650-2 (e)

CONTENTS

ACKNOWLEDGEMENTS

Although my contributions as an author have been minor, my wife, Darlene, my daughter, Sheri, and my son, Craig {who is a Commander in the United States Navy} have all encouraged me to write a sequel to *MOST UNCOMMON EVENTS AT RYAN PARK. Without their assistance and confidence I would never have attempted to write this sequel. As well, I wish to thank Tina Hill, manager of the Old Frontier Prison in Rawlins, Wyoming especially for her interest in maintaining the old prison in such excellent condition. Tina digs deep into Wyoming's prison history to bring many forgotten aspects of the old prison and prison history in general so as to enhance the public's awareness.*

ABOUT THE AUTHOR AND THE BOOK

Duane Shillinger grew up on the Crow Indian Reservation near Wyola and Lodge Grass, Montana. Life on the reservation was difficult with meager amounts of money for his parents to provide for the basic needs of the family members. Duane attended an Indian school at Wyola and achieved poorly in the multi-cultural environment. His mother, acutely aware of the poor academic achievement, found it possible for the family to move to Sheridan, Wyoming where Duane was exposed to new opportunities.

After graduating from high school, Duane enlisted in the United States Navy and was assigned to a communication station for the Sixth Fleet in North Africa. Later, Duane was assigned to several ships where he served as a radioman. He very much enjoyed using Morse Code as a means to send messages.

Once out of the Navy Duane attended the Sheridan Community College and then graduated from the University of Wyoming, majoring in social work and psychology.

In 1967 Duane was employed at the Wyoming State Penitentiary as a counselor and was eventually appointed as Deputy Warden; and, in 1979, Governor Edward Herschler appointed Duane to serve as Warden of the prison. After nearly thirty (30) years' service at the prison, Duane retired and he and his wife, Darlene, located in the small community of Ryan Park, a summer and retirement home located above Saratoga, Wyoming.

It was at Ryan Park that Duane was inspired by the environment and sometimes the clash of residents to try his hand at writing a mystery novel. His book, MOST UNCOMMON EVENTS AT RYAN PARK, left two (2) characters believing that Irana Dubliski was wrongly released from the charge of murdering her husband.

COYOTE AND MAGPIE re-examines the murder charge and, often under difficult conditions, collects information that will be used during a new trial. Involved in the quest for new information and eventual justice are Deputy Sheriff Lenny Craig and citizen Delmar Mentis who take the reader along with them as they investigate every aspect of the crime that they believe was committed by Irana Dubliski.

As evidence is collected, Deputy Craig and Delmar Mentis convince Sheriff Chester Overman and Judge Wolfe that the ultimate sentence be given to Irana Dubliski. "Debts" due from certain legislators enable the law enforcement group to carry out an unusual punishment at the old, vacated prison. Strange legal and quasi legal machinations are not uncommon in Wyoming and although this is a purely fictional possibility, that very possibility of using the old prison during an actual case was discussed in 1992.

What will Deputy Craig and Delmar Mentis achieve in their investigation and court room drama? What event awaits the defendant, Irana Dubliski at the old prison? We shall see as COYOTE AND MAPIE is read.

COYOTE AND MAGPIE

In the Wyoming State prison an incarcerated American Indian composed a poem about a coyote and a magpie. Possibly inspired by his own anxieties and discomfort with his environment the Native American wrote of the journey of a coyote and a magpie as they searched for food. That poem was given to the author of COYOTE AND MAGPIE and it was placed on a wall in the warden's office where it remained for many years.

Now, the essence of that poem is used as a means to focus on and emphasize the efforts of the two men who have been charged with fully investigating the deaths of Gregorio Dubliski and Deputy Sheriff Clem Sours. As well, the poem serves as excellent foreshadowing.

We first see coyote and magpie as they wend their way along the Yellowstone and Musselshell rivers, along the banks of these rivers where tall grasses grow. With winter in full force, the grass is blown at rakish angles, flattened with snow and ice. They see the tracks and droppings of the buffalo: their prey. Over hills and valleys they follow the trail. Wind and snow makes their quest difficult. The magpie soars above the slower moving coyote but not beyond him as the magpie knows that the coyote will deliver the first blow.

Then the herd of brown, ice covered buffalo are spotted. They have grown shaggy. Their faces dripping gold at sunrise when they drink. The magpie thinks: our medicine is not always strong. Feathers lose their brilliance and fray with too much handling. Brother, you are Coyote in your song and I am Magpie with no hands, drifting, staying here all winter without color.

The buffalo have found open ground not far from the Yellowstone. Ice covers their long beards; their bodies worn fatigued from their endless journey. Snot and spittle adorns the hair on their skulls. As would be expected, the magpie spots the herd first. He propels himself down ward as if to communicate a message to the coyote. The wind tosses and pulls at his feathers. Below, the coyote has scented the herd. He is near his limit in the energy that will be necessary to pull down one of the shaggy beasts. On toward the herd came the magpie and the coyote, both nearly at their end of their endurance.

Steadily walking and trotting through the tall grass and occasional sage brush they spotted the herd on the slope of a small hill. Wind and snow swept their tails as if they were swatting summer flies. Stopping and lowering himself in a crouch, the coyote carefully examined each member of the herd. Then, with almost silent growls and whimpers, the coyote selected his prey. It was a female, a cow of maybe two years. The magpie knew the reason for this selection because the cow slowly limped behind the moving herd. A crippled cow: something that the coyote could bring down onto the snow and ice. The magpie readied himself for the bloody event soon to occur.

Moving slowly so as to not alarm the limping cow, the coyote made a series of fast runs, always keeping his belly close to the ground. At times the coyote would make an oblique run toward the cow, going to the left of her and then to the right. All designed to confuse the beast in the event that she had now spotted the grey creature moving closer and closer to her. When she did realize what was creeping upon her, she attempted an evasive run toward the herd that was now some distance from her. The coyote saw that the cow was now limping to the extent that she was nearly dragging a rear leg. She would not reach the protection of the herd. Above, the magpie watched in anticipation. He dove and soared, using the wind to propel himself, but never allowing himself to fly beyond the spectacle below.

Finally, the coyote was within reach of the cow. She knew he was there: her eyes bulged; her rib cage heaved as she grunted and groaned; she snorted snot and foam--all the while most likely knowing the events awaiting her. The coyote stopped; dropped to its belly; and waited. He was resting; building up the strength he knew would be necessary for him to complete each element of the kill. When the time came, the coyote sprang forward and with teeth bared caught the cow's tail. The force of the little grey animal threw the cow to one side, almost bringing her to the ground.

The coyote released the animal and watched as it attempted to regain its balance. Now was the time for bolder attack. The coyote threw itself at one of the cow's legs. Teeth bared, the lunge brought the coyote in contact with one of the cow's legs: this time flesh was pulled from the point of impact. The cow buffalo bawled loudly and jerked away from the coyote. With a mass of hair and bloody meat in its mouth, the coyote intensified its attack. The next lunge at the cow brought her to her knees. Her grunts and bawling caused members of the herd, at some distance now, to stop and turn toward her. Realizing what was taking place, the herd slowly turned and, with heads bent low, made their way against the wind and blowing snow.

Another lunge by the coyote delivered a serious wound to the cow's leg. She was now on her side, kicking and pawing at the coyote. Avoiding the sharp hoofs, the coyote tore at the cow's throat. The coyote's sharp teeth drew a heavy spurt of blood. The cow was entering its final attempt at self-preservation. Blood soaked the snow-covered earth; blood dripped from the frozen grass; the frozen snow and foam on her skull turned pink, then red. She protruded her tongue in agony, bleating and groaning. Grabbing the extended tongue between his teeth the coyote ripped the tongue from the cow's mouth. Now in a feeding rage the coyote intensified its kill instincts. The cow now lay nearly quiet, except for involuntary trembling and jerking. It was over. The magpie slowly fluttered down and sat upon one of the cow's horns. The magpie thought: "I will sit on a horn and scream. I cannot eat until the pain is over, the flesh quits moving, and the smell is dead…"

CHAPTER ONE
EARLY SPRING... AT RYAN PARK

Wind and snow slashing against the bed room window awakened Delmar Mentis from his deep sleep. It was a noisy storm and Delmar, once awake, was again disappointed with the weather. He wished for spring: a spring with quick snow melt; a spring with warm breezes; a spring that would enable him to begin the hunt for evidence necessary to convict Irana Dubliski of the murder of her husband.

But spring at Ryan Park came in stages. The first stage being the spring snows: heavy wet, often deep snow. Following stages involved the snow melt and mud. He would just have to wait, especially he would wait for the meeting with Deputy Sheriff Lenny Craig.

He removed the heavy down quilt and slid out of bed, careful to not disturb Rhonda. At the window he stopped to view the storm that raged outside his well- built cabin. Unable to see beyond the window sill he satisfied himself by watching the wind and snow lash at the once well- made web fashioned by a cat spider that had made a home at a corner of the window. Soon, as he watched, the web was in shreds and the skeleton of the cat spider—all that remained of the little spider—was blown from the window by a gust of wind. The cat spider had died during the first on-set of cold weather: all she left was her skeleton and an egg sack that she had carefully created and then, with her special chemicals, had adhered it to a small protected corner of the window. Delmar marveled at the strength of the egg sack as it withstood the beating of the storm. As the temperature would eventually warm, if Delmar happened to be nearby to watch the event, thousands of cat spider eggs would emerge into thousands of tiny spiders. Warm winds would lift the baby spiders into the air with destinations unknown. Delmar knew that, at the right time, if he looked carefully about his house he would find another cat spider web and a secluded mother spider lying in wait for a moth or a fly to become entangled in her web.

As he turned from the window the bone-chilling sound of coyotes stopped his progress to the kitchen. He returned to the window and peered into the inky darkness. Out there in the storm, probably somewhere at the base of Barrett Ridge, were the coyotes. Delmar thought the howls, barks, and yips he heard were being made by three coyotes…and they were on the hunt.

He followed the coyotes as they marked their progress along the ridge with their howls and yips. Delmar knew when they turned and began to retrace their routes. Then the intensity of the howls and barks alerted Delmar to know that they had found their prey. As their howls and yips continued to shatter the darkness, Delmar could only imagine the painful plight of the unfortunate victim. Death would be quick; the coyotes' proficiency would ensure a quick end. The prey? A new spring fawn? Perhaps just a rabbit? Or some feathered fowl? Whatever it was, the meal would be far too meager for three coyotes: they would soon be on the hunt again. A wise animal would remain frozen in its tracks as the coyotes needed little movement of any kind to draw their attention.

It was quiet now. Delmar made his way from the window and toward the kitchen, but not before bumping into the bed.

"Is that you, Delmar?" came a sleepy voice.

"Well, ahhh yeah" mumbled Delmar. "Who else would it be?" he snickered.

"Okay, smarty," Rhonda quickly answered, well understanding his almost concealed remark. "What are you doing up anyway?" she asked.

"Oh, the coyotes woke me up. So, I thought I would go out and get me a hot chocolate or something. Can I get you anything?" he asked.

"You best get back in bed and get some sleep if you still plan to meet Lenny Craig in the morning," Rhonda admonished.

Delmar, counting on his awareness of furniture in the bed room, proceeded to the bed room door without bumping into any other objects, and made his way to the kitchen.

After placing the tea pot on a stove burner, Delmar sat at the dining room table and waited for the sharp whistle that would tell him the water was ready. Once that alarm sounded, Delmar, not wanting to further waken Rhonda, quickly made his way to the stove to silence the noisy pot. As he poured the hot water into his favorite mug he decided upon hot chocolate rather than tea. Perhaps hot chocolate would put an end to his sleepless activities. Sipping the hot chocolate, he began to consider the agenda that he would present to Lenny Craig. It had been a long winter with more than ample time to consider all of the events that had occurred before and after Irana Dubliski had left Carbon County. Several times during the winter he and Lenny Craig had discussed their feelings and ideas about Irana Dubliski and their suspicions that she was the instigator of the death of her husband, Gregorio Dublisk;, and that she may well have been responsible for the death of Deputy Clem Sours. Lenny Craig and Delmar had decided to meet on May 19, tomorrow morning, to outline their investigative strategy. With the mug of hot chocolate empty, Delmar made his way back to the bedroom hoping to get some sleep before the meeting with Lenny.

CHAPTER TWO

IRANA DUBLISKI

Fear had replaced her normal thoughts and her thoughts now centered entirely on the best choices she had to try to avoid the arrest that she knew was looming before her. At first she had been confident that her activities had been sufficient to totally distance herself from the death of her husband, Gregorio Dubliski; but as time passed and as she had relived the events leading up to the death of her husband she became increasingly aware of the small mistakes that she had made: mistakes that an astute investigator would quickly detect. Mindful of these small errors, she traced and retraced all of her activities that night when the time came for her to once and for all rid herself of the man who had mistreated her for so many years. Perhaps the most repulsive event of that night was the manner in which she had dispatched Sheriff Deputy Clem Sours. Although she had been certain at the time of his death that his demise would be considered a suicide, her confidence in that belief had begun to diminish. As she struggled with her thoughts, often trying to reassure herself that all would be well, she found herself beginning to believe that it was not so much the concerns she had about any mistakes that she had made, but more about just the feelings of guilt that she had to admit were beginning to confuse her initial attempts to avoid detection.

Avoiding detection and arrest, she decided, had to be her primary focus. To achieve this goal, Irana had changed her name to Nora Dolor. She found a new apartment and different employment, hoping to totally erase any traces of Irana Dubliski. She had wanted to leave Omaha but she did not have the funds necessary to relocate and reestablish herself. She would have to take her chances and just hope that she could not be located.

It was now a matter of trying to allay her fears, yet knowing that back in Carbon County there were serious efforts underway to assemble the facts that would support a warrant for her arrest.

Nora Dolor found her stability weakened and her behavioral foundation crumbling. She was tense. She was dominated by anxiety. She was paranoid. She became suspicious of people who looked at her on the street. She was constantly on guard: waiting for the arrival of the lawmen from Carbon County.

CHAPTER THREE

THE MEETING

Heavy, dark clouds lay over Ryan Park; and from those clouds wet snow greeted Delmar as he peered from a window of his cabin. Today was the day for which he had been waiting. The new snows did not dampen the excitement he felt, and his mind was ever busy arranging the issues that he had thoroughly and painstakingly examined throughout the long winter. He gulped down the coffee that Rhonda had placed before him and finished a pancake and a side of scrambled eggs. It was almost time to leave the cabin and meet Deputy Sheriff Lenny Craig.

"I guess there is nothing I can say that would perhaps change your mind about all of this?" Rhonda asked as she continued placing freshly washed dishes in the storage area above the kitchen sink. She knew the answer to her question, but felt obligated to at least ask it.

"No, my dear....I know that you have reservations about my interest in this issue, but since I was the one who found the body...since you and I served on the Coroner's jury...since there are so many unanswered questions...well, I just have to see this thing through. I have such strong feelings that this Irana Dubliski was involved up to her teeth that I am absolutely compelled to do what I can to assist Lenny Craig." Delmar answered, hoping to allay her doubts and gain her support.

"I have some strong feelings as well, Delmar..." Rhonda paused giving thought to her rebuttal, "...neither you nor I know how this will all end. I don't know Irana Dubliski and I don't know if she is guilty, but she is a person. It is almost as if you and Lenny are tracking some type of animal. Wouldn't it be best to just let this alone? I have terrible feelings that this will not end well..."

"Can't do that, Rhonda...." Delmar quickly responded. "Maybe she is innocent…maybe not. Lenny and I are just trying to put all of the facts together so that a final decision can be made. No, she is not an animal… but, if she did somehow murder her husband then she should be held accountable. Then, there is also the issue of how Deputy Clem Sours died. There was something going on between the two of them, and his death seems awful suspicious. Anyway, the death of a law enforcement official just can't be ignored. If it was suicide, so be it. If it was murder then…. well you know the rest…"

"You best get going," Rhonda answered, "Lenny will be waiting for you. Be careful and always keep your focus on what lays ahead…"

"Hmmm, that sounds sort of cryptic, Rhonda. I'll try to figure that all out later. Anyway, my focus is to just try to help Lenny. I feel obligated now after he asked me if I would like to be part of this investigation, which, I might add, has the blessings of the sheriff."

Delmar gave Rhonda a quick peck on the cheek, and then he was on his way to the café. His pickup splashed through the wet accumulating snow, snow that now nearly covered the gravel road. Once at the café he carefully guided his pickup to an empty parking place, and then began walking to the café entrance. He noted that Deputy Craig's vehicle was already parked. Inside the café, Delmar spotted Deputy Craig sitting at a far table next to the row of windows on the north side of the room.

"Hello, Deputy and good morning to you," Delmar loudly greeted the Deputy Craig.

"Morning, Delmar…" Lenny softly answered. "I don't have much time as I have another issue that I need to attend to, but we have time to go over our plans for this summer…that is if summer ever arrives."

"Sounds fine to me," Delmar answered. "let me order some coffee and a donut or two."

As they waited for the coffee and pastries Deputy Craig again emphasized the importance of the approval for the investigation as given by both the sheriff and the County Attorney. Lenny mentioned that the sheriff had suggested a rudimentary course for the investigation and that they would follow those suggestions while also adding their own ideas and plans of action. With hot coffee in the mugs before them and several fresh pastries waiting to be eaten, Deputy Craig and Lenny, armed with pencils and pads of paper, readied themselves for the long- awaited discussion that would center squarely on Irana Dubliski.

"Obviously, we are not going to delve into any analysis of evidence today," Lenny began, "...so, let's just lay out a plan that will help us analyze any available evidence and, as well, a plan that will hopefully lead us in the direction of additional evidence." Looking out the window Lenny offered a grumpy summary of how the weather will probably impede their out of doors activities. "So, Delmar," Lenny continued, "let's start with a visit to the Forest Ranger who has had the remains of the bear in a safe keeping spot. We need to carefully examine what remains of the bear...I'm not sure that we will find anything that we don't already have, but it's a place to start. Probably, we need to take additional photos; do some measurements of what is left of the carcass; and maybe collect several samples for analysis. We will need to prove to a jury that the bear was transported to our area illegally; and we need to demonstrate how we believe the bear killed Gregorio Dubliski....with a few comments as to how we believe the bear was trained to kill this fellow." Deputy Craig paused and jotted several notes on his pad of paper.

Taking the opportunity to speak while Lenny was occupied with his notes, Delmar offered that "...another issue that I believe needs to be examined is the trailer. Except for a very cursory examination I don't think there was a really good inspection of the trailer. Where is it now, anyway?"

"I have been keeping track of the trailer since it was moved from the Forest Service camp ground; and, as far as I know, it still remains in the County impound lot. To my knowledge no one has been in or around the trailer. Good idea. We need to go over it inch by inch," Lenny answered.

"If and when the snow stops..." Lenny paused as he again looked out the window to view the falling heavy wet snow, "...and the snow melts; and the ground dries up a tad, we need to get out with metal-detectors and comb that area where the bear carcass was found. If we could find the bullet...better, if we could find the bear's skull with the bullet inside we would be on a roll, especially if we could find the gun that was used to kill the bear."

"A lot of IFS in that, Lenny," Delmar smiled as he acknowledged the direction Lenny was taking. "But, yes...maybe a little luck will lead us in some of that direction."

Taking a big swig of his coffee, Lenny idly twirled his pencil while often tapping the tip of the pencil on his writing pad. "Let's take a moment and think about our agenda so far and also give serious thought to any other issue that we can examine…there may be some other issues that we have not even considered."

"One thing, and I may be way off the mark on this, but there is the death of Clem Sours that just does not ring right with me," Delmar spoke as if talking to no one. "I didn't know Clem well at all, but from the little that I knew of him he just did not seem the type to take his own life. You…," Delmar paused and pointed his pencil at Lenny, "…are the one who might be able to make any sense of the few facts that have been collected about his death."

"I'm not even certain that I know of a starting point on that," Lenny responded. "How do you go about proving that a suicide was not a suicide when the coroner has ruled the death a suicide? Any way we will re-examine his pickup; go through all of his property; walk through the area where his pickup was found; and maybe, just maybe find something that may yield a clue."

"Anything else that you can think of?" Lenny asked before taking another long drink of his coffee.

Pausing before making his suggestion, Delmar carefully considered how he would broach the subject. "Well, Deputy," he paused again, "…this may be way off base, but I am wondering if we should bring Irana Dubliski back here and interrogate her again?"

Lenny answered immediately, tapping his pen on his note pad as if to give emphasis to his answer. "No…I have already asked the Sheriff that same question and I was told that it is far too early to contact her in any way, shape, or form. The Sheriff said that once we have discovered significant facts then, at that time, we can plan on how we should approach her." Continuing, Lenny thoughtfully provided his own assessment of contacting Irana Dubliski too early in the investigation. "We don't want to spook her. If she runs to a new location we may have a very difficult time finding her. At this time we pretty much know where she is located."

"I agree with that," Delmar answered. "We certainly don't want to spook her."

"Anything else that you can think of, Delmar?" Deputy Craig asked.

"I have two more stops that I need to make this morning, so, if there is nothing more to add to our agenda, best get on about the rest of the day."

"Again," Delmar began, "I know that this is not even a consideration, but I will toss it out there anyway. I wonder just how unethical it would be to interview Dubliski's attorney, Constance Meaning."

"Attorney/client privileges are pretty sacred," Lenny answered, giving thought to the suggestion. "However, if we can prove to Constance that Dubliski was untruthful as she defended Dubliski, that may just pave the way for Constance to open up a bit….let's keep that in mind as we proceed."

"If there is nothing else, Delmar, I need to hit the road and take care of some other issues," Lenny reminded Delmar.

"No, can't think of anything more," Delmar answered quickly. "So, I guess our next meeting will be at the Forest Service to examine what's left of the bear…."

"Yup," Lenny answered. "I'll give you a call and we can make arrangements. I will bring my cameras and other essentials"

As the Deputy moved from the table, Delmar offered to pay for the coffee and donuts, "Okay, Deputy, I'll be waiting for your call."

As Lenny walked to the door, he offered a final comment: "you probably have more money than me anyhow….see ya…"

Grey skies and falling snow greeted Delmar as he left the café. By the time he reached his pickup snow covered the brim of his hat and the shoulders of his heavy coat.

CHAPTER FOUR

WAITING FOR THE WEEKEND

At the computer store, Delmar's place of work in Laramie, he half-heartedly organized his work day schedule. There were several computers to repair and a list of customers with questions to call. As he impatiently prepared to begin his daily chores, he suddenly found himself thinking of that day in May, now nearly a year ago.

He had been on his morning jog….the weather was perfect that day. As he entered a small grove of aspen trees he noticed several magpies flitting from tree to tree. Although he had often seen magpies during his morning run, this morning the black and white birds seemed edgy as if something nearby caused them alarm. He gave them little thought as he continued his way along the old logging trail. Soon, his attention shifted to a porcupine that occupied the better part of the trail. Slowing to a walk, he recalled edging by the rodent, and then regained his normal pace. Just a few yards beyond the porcupine he recalled noticing a hunting knife lying at the edge of the trail. Dropping to his knees he carefully examined the knife, wondering why it was lying here at the particular place. The knife, he recalled, was not rusty, as it would have been had it been lying here all winter. And then he realized that the knife most likely belonged to Tony Foyt. Picking up the knife and placing it in his belly-pack, he continued on his way.

Reaching for the cup of coffee that he had placed nearby, he paused again to reflect upon the next chain of events that he encountered that morning. As he rounded a small curve in the trail the pines and aspen became less dense: he was able to clearly view the trail as it began a gradual slope downward to eventually connect with the Forest Service road. He recalled thinking that his morning run was nearly completed and that he would soon be back at his cabin in Ryan Park and then on his way to work in Laramie. It was not to be. Delmar then recalled seeing what appeared to be a body lying on the trail. After determining that the body was that of a man and that the man was deceased, he quickly left the area; increased his running speed; arrived at his cabin; and immediately telephoned Deputy Lenny Craig.

Delmar smiled as thoughts of the Coroner's jury entered his mind. He clearly remembered Dr. Purdy, the cigar smoking Coroner with his sly wit. As well, he could still see Rhonda as she vomited when Dr. Purdy removed the sheet covering the John Doe who awaited the surgical knife used by Dr. Purdy. Delmar then recalled that it was he who identified the metal arrow point that Dr. Purdy removed from John Doe's back. The arrow that had been attached to the metal point was later found by Delmar and Deputy Craig. When the arrow and other evidence were found not far from where the body lay on the trail, it was quite clear that the John Doe, later identified as Gregorio Dubliski, was the victim of the act of murder.

With thoughts of that day in May, a year ago, still lingering, Delmar's efforts returned to his work. That afternoon, however, as the end of his work day neared, he drifted back to the events associated with the body of the dead man he found. What exactly did he know for certain? Tapping a small screw driver that he held on the work table, Delmar began to mentally tally the facts that had been thus far determined: the dead man had been murdered; an arrow had been violently inserted into his back and into his heart; Deputy Lenny Craig was certain that a trained bear had delivered the arrow; evidence-- (including a broken arrow, pieces of burlap sack that had probably been wrapped about shoes and even the paws of the bear to eliminate the presence of shoe and paw tracks; an abandoned trailer that had been used to transport a bear; and the untimely death of Deputy Clem Sours who was known to have associated with Irana Dubliski)— found near the crime scene fully supported the belief that someone, in addition to the trained bear, was fully involved in the murder.

Following the work day, on his way back to Ryan Park, Delmar re-examined the known evidence and wondered to what degree the evidence would play in a trial setting. The prosecuting attorney would be obligated to prove exactly who had trained the bear to deliver the arrow; and, equally important, the prosecuting attorney would need to prove that the person who had trained the bear was the same person who had orchestrated the murder. Thus, the prosecuting attorney must prove that the person who had trained the bear was the same person who had transported the bear to the site of the murder and had also made the preparations necessary to conceal, destroy, and confuse evidence.

Delmar, as were those in law enforcement agencies, was certain that Irana Dubliski, the wife of the murder victim, was the very person who had trained the bear to deliver the fatal arrow. Proving that assumption in court would depend upon the proven credibility of the known evidence as well as other evidence that yet may become available.

Then, there was the death of Deputy Clem Sours—a death initially attributed to suicide. Those in law enforcement did not accept that suicide was the cause of death. Again, how to prove that Irana Dubliski was somehow responsible for the deputy's death was an obstacle to adding the charge of murder of a law enforcement official to the charge of the murder of her husband.

Throughout the remaining days of the week Delmar puzzled and mulled over the evidence associated with the murder. It would not be long now, as winter snows were quickly melting away. Signs of spring were becoming apparent throughout Ryan Park: willows were leafing out, mountain flowers were popping up here and there, aspen trees were beginning to leaf, and muddy roads were drying and passable. Spring had arrived and with it the quest for evidence. The coyote and magpie would soon be on the hunt.

The time had arrived: Delmar Mentis and Deputy Lenny Craig's work lay before them. As they prepared for their hunt for evidence, what would their prey, Irana Dubliski, be doing to prevent detection and arrest?

CHAPTER FIVE

NORA DOLOR

She well understood that she was the center of attention—the primary target in the investigation of her husband's murder. Irana Dubliski, now Nora Dolor, had begun to associate her plight as a person wanted for murder with that of a hunted animal.

Her attempts to convince herself that she was merely creating unnecessary thoughts and worries about her arrest and return to Carbon County were unsuccessful. To control her anxiety and constant fears she had begun to use alcohol. She had lost interest in her employment, but quitting her job was not an option. She had few friends now—most of her friends had observed her withdrawal from social activities and normal social exchanges.

Nora was aware that the good looks that had once attracted Deputy Clem Sours were being replaced by lines of anxiety and worry. Mentally and physically she was fast losing her ability to maintain even simple responsibilities. Would she be able to regain her composure and some sense of normalcy were she simply to decide to render a confession when the time came? That thought remained constant and surfaced following bouts of anxiety and worry.

CHAPTER SIX
EXAMINING THE BEAR CARCASS

Finally, the day had arrived for the examination of the bear carcass. Delmar had arisen early that morning. A quick breakfast, a parting hug with Rhonda, and he was out of the cabin. A glance at his wrist watch convinced him that he would arrive before Lenny Craig. Guiding his Ford Bronco into the drive way leading to the Forestry office where the bear carcass was being held, he was surprised to see that Deputy Craig had arrived first.

Lenny Craig waited by his Carbon County Sheriff's Department pick-up. Lenny was handsomely dressed in his uniform—sun glasses added a professional appearance.

"Mornin' Delmar," Lenny offered the first salutation.

"Howdy, Lenny," Delmar answered. "I was going to try to arrive here first, but as usual you were Johnny on the spot."

"Well, let's get at it. The Forest ranger gave me the key to that building yonder. That's where they have stored the bear." Lenny directed Delmar to the place where they would examine the bear.

The pair walked the short distance to the building. Lenny opened the door and as they entered they were greeted by a damp, musty odor. The well insulated building was cool and fairly well ventilated. Conditions, the Forest department believed, that were more than adequate for the proper maintenance of the bear carcass.

"Okay," Lenny began, "what we need to do is photograph the carcass and take some samples for DNA analysis. Also, while I am doing those two tasks, I want you to take this tape measure and carefully measure the dimensions of the carcass. Accurately record your measurements."

The carcass of the bear was resting on a make-shift table, about three feet above the floor. "Not much of him is left, is there?" Delmar assessed.

"Nope, this ole boy has seen better days, for sure," Lenny answered. "Well, let's get at it and get out to some better smelling air."

Photographs were taken: samples of dried flesh, bone, and hair were carefully removed and properly recorded and placed in sample collection containers. "I got good pics," Lenny began, "I tried to think about what a jury would want to see. So, I made sure that the entire carcass would be shown. Also, photos of the place where the skull would have been attached and the leg that still has the metal cup attached will be beneficial to a jury. The photo of that metal cuff will be important to a jury because that will demonstrate exactly how the arrow was delivered."

"And," Lenny continued, "good DNA evidence will be important to convince a jury that the bear was transported by the Dubliskis from Michigan."

"I suspect that you will use a reliable and recognized DNA lab?" Delmar asked.

"Oh, you bet," Lenny responded. "Everything will be professionally processed, certified, and prepared for evidence."

"What about the photographs?" Delmar posed. "A defense lawyer could raise doubts about the importance of the photos, and even attempt to discredit the validity of them," Delmar continued.

Lenny thought for a moment and said "…well, I will have the crime lab develop the photos, and I will have a sworn statement from the Forest Department attesting to the discovery, analysis, and secure storage of the carcass. There will be a very good chain of evidence presented to the jury. There should be no doubt about the carcass itself or about the photos and DNA evidence."

Lenny and Delmar walked around the table where the carcass lay, looking for any further evidence that should be collected and recorded.

"Well, I guess that's it," Lenny summed up their work. "Can't think of anything else here that we can collect."

"Guess not," Delmar agreed, "…thinking ahead, if we can just find the skull we maybe can find evidence that the bear was intentionally killed."

"Absolutely," Lenny chimed in. "the bear skull is vital to prove that some one killed the bear to conceal how the murder was committed. In fact, get your metal detector ready. I am planning to begin the hunt for the bear skull and, hopefully, a bullet…say…tomorrow if the weather holds."

"I'll be ready," Delmar answered with obvious eagerness.

The pair exited the storage building and walked to the ranger's office. There Deputy Craig thanked the ranger for the assistance and mentioned the need for the official statement regarding the bear and it's discovery. That document was immediately given to Lenny.

Once reaching their vehicles, Deputy Craig informed Delmar that tomorrow he would be at the place where the bear was discovered. "Soon as we get to the place where the bear was found we can begin the search for the skull and a bullet." And with that Delmar chimed in, "I'll be there."

CHAPTER SEVEN
SEARCHING FOR A BEAR'S SKULL

Just a few fluffy clouds drifted above Ryan Park that early May Sunday morning. Delmar had risen early and prepared himself for the search. Rhonda served up a big breakfast and prepared a lunch that he would enjoy later in the day.

"Guess I can't convince you to not get any further involved in this investigation?" Rhonda quietly asked, well knowing Delmar's answer. She had been opposed to his involvement in the issue, but hesitated to overly impose herself.

"No," Delmar responded, "I am just too darn psyched-up...I guess that's the best way to describe my feelings. That woman killed her husband, and I became involved the day that I found his body."

They sat quietly then as breakfast and coffee occupied their time. Rhonda, offering no further comments to dissuade Delmar, encouraged him to be safe and to enjoy the day. With a farewell hug and a kiss on the cheek, Delmar left the cabin and stood for a moment on the deck, relishing in the new spring day. Already the sun had removed the chill of the previous night; several blue jays flirted about in search of a morning meal; and the faint sound of Barrett Creek—now free of ice and snow drifts—bubbling below the cabin could be heard.

Driving the short distance to the road near the location where the bear had been found, Delmar gave thought to the manner in which he and Deputy Craig would search for the skull and bullet. As he entered a curve in the road he saw Deputy Craig's pick-up. Lenny was removing his metal detector and necessary gear to be used to process the items they were hoping to find.

Parking his vehicle behind Lenny's pick-up, Delmar removed his metal detector and walked the short distance to greet Lenny. "Hello and good morning," Delmar loudly shouted. Looks like you have everything you need to find that skull."

"'Bout as ready as I can get, I guess," was Lenny's response.

With metal detectors and other gear in hand, the two began walking toward the area where the bear had been found. Deputy Craig suddenly slowed his gait, then stopped. "Let me take a moment and give you an update," Lenny began. "While you were at work last week, I did some snooping around—and what I learned may well shed additional light on Irana Dubliski's activities the day or night that her husband was murdered. Along with what I discovered I formed a few opinions that I will let you mull over. To begin, I spoke with several people who were at the restaurant on the evening of April 30, 1982. I was told that they saw a vehicle –they couldn't exactly describe the color as it was late evening—but it appeared to be a dark color. And, of particular interest, the vehicle was pulling a white trailer. Again, they were uncertain, but it looked like two people were in the vehicle."

"Then," Lenny continued, "...about an hour or so later, they saw the same vehicle drive past the restaurant, but this time it was not attached to the trailer. Now, and this is a shocker, around 11 o'clock, they saw a black pick-up turn off the highway, drive past the restaurant, and continue up the road. Later, maybe half an hour or a little longer, the black pick-up again drove past the restaurant, but this time it was pulling a white trailer."

"A black pick-up?" Delmar interrupted. "Holy wind storm! Deputy Clem Sours owned a black pick-up—a GMC."

"You bet he did," Lenny quickly affirmed. "Let's just suppose that Sours was up here helping the Dubliski woman—for whatever reason we don't know—but if that was him and she was with him, that could well connect her to his death."

"Deputy, you deserve a medal," Delmar stated as he gave Lenny a pat on the back. "So," he continued, "will that info be suitable for court?"

"Absolutely," Lenny answered, "I have the witness statements recorded and I have written, notarized affidavits. The witnesses said they would gladly testify in court."

"There are several issues that most likely occurred just prior to or following the death of Dubliski"s victim. For example, we don't fully understand why she pulled the trailer up here and then left the area without the trailer. The trailer is well linked to the bear; so, we can rightfully suspect that the trailer was used to pull the bear up here. More on that in a bit. We also don't know why Deputy Sours, if that was him, came up here and then left the area pulling the trailer. It is my suspicion that the Dubliski woman pulled the trailer that contained the bear to the place just below where you found the body. For whatever reason, again just suspicion, the victim left the car and walked up the logging trail; the woman released the bear and the bear, as it was trained, found the victim and delivered the arrow into the victim's back. The bear returned through the willows and brush just beyond where we are now standing. Then, again just conjecture, the Dubliski woman pulled the trailer up to the place where the bear exited the willows; she loaded the bear back into the trailer; and she then deliberately eased the car and trailer into the ditch next to the road bed."

"I know that I am really pushing facts here, but without some attempt to understand what took place we will never get to the truth. So, by posing some possibilities, testing them, and looking for other possibilities we may create a pretty good picture of what exactly took place that night. Let me continue with my opinions: once the trailer was in the ditch, she unhooked the car; left the trailer; and drove back to the cabin that they had rented. There, at the cabin, she telephoned Deputy Sours and told him that she needed help removing the trailer from the ditch. She left her car at the cabin and walked the distance back to the trailer to wait for Sours. The distance wasn't that far, maybe two miles."

Continuing, Lenny added: "Why she wanted Sours there at the trailer we can't be certain. Maybe, at that point, she knew that she had to rid herself of the bear to further cover the cause of her husband's death and she felt that she needed someone to assist in this part of her scheme. Or, maybe, and this is a big leap…maybe she believed that Sours knew too much about her and she feared that he was on the verge of reporting her to his superiors. So, luring Sours to the trailer…all the while pretending that the trailer was mired down and she needed help removing it from the ditch…was the perfect way to place him in a position where she could make certain that he talked to no one again."

"My head is reeling," Delmar began, "you have really put some thought into this and it is my opinion that you may actually have created a plausible explanation of what actually occurred."

"Let me go a bit further, and this is a little ragged in terms of a factual occurrence of events." Lenny then began to describe his opinions of what took place following Deputy Sours' arrival at the trailer. "Most likely, once Sours was at the trailer, the Dubliski woman gave him a song and dance as to what she was doing in the area and why the trailer was in the ditch without the car attached. She probably asked him to remove the trailer from the ditch, which he did by hooking his pick-up to the trailer and pulling the trailer from the ditch. Then, she asked him to turn his pick-up and trailer around and pull the trailer back to her cabin. The road being narrow and leading away from Ryan Park, gave Sours no alternative but to back the trailer into a side road, an old logging road. She then stopped Sours from going further--probably telling him that she needed to check something in the trailer. She then walked to the rear of the trailer; opened the door; removed the bear; walked it to the edge of the road and a little beyond; and, at that point, she shot the bear and quickly covered it with the timber slag that was readily available. She then entered the pick-up with Sours and asked him to pull the trailer back to her cabin. From that point we just don't know what took place. We need to come up with more possibilities, but, again just conjecture, Sours was entering his last living hours."

"There you have it, Delmar. That is what I have come up with. We need to pick it apart and try to find additional explanations for what occurred that night. Irana Dubliski has left her tracks and we are starting to really pick-up on the scent. Like coyotes after an old rabbit we are very near to our prey. Anyway, here we are in the middle of this old muddy road, just yards away from where the bear was found. We best head up there and get started. Let me get my GPS out and find our exact position. Once we get to about where the bear was found I'll establish exact GPS coordinates and compare them with the coordinates given to me by the Forest Service."

"On up the road we need to go," Lenny directed. "I want to stop for a minute up there and take a look at about where we think the bear came out of the willows."

When they reached the place that Lenny had mentioned, they stopped and Lenny detailed yet another speculation regarding Irana Dubliski's activities. "We are just about below the place where we found the broken arrow and the pieces of burlap...it was also there that you found what appeared to be a foot print bearing the mesh imprint of burlap. Most likely the bear lost those items as he charged through the willows and brush. I believe that the woman had pulled or was pulling the trailer to this spot at about the time the bear entered the road. She most likely loaded the bear into the trailer just about where we are now standing."

Lenny paused for several moments—turning to look back down the road and then turning toward the willows—as if trying to visualize what took place once Irana Dubliski pulled the trailer to the place where they now stood. "Most likely...and I keep saying most likely..." he continued, "it was about here that she disconnected her vehicle from the trailer and then drove back down past the restaurant. She would have had to walk back here, once she left her car—probably at the cabin that they had rented—and here, next to the trailer, she waited for Deputy Sours...if that was actually him..."

"Maybe," Delmar interrupted, "she didn't walk back here. Is it possible that Deputy Sours could have been waiting for her, and when she arrived he drove her back to the trailer?"

"Well, that is a possibility," Lenny answered, "and we will keep that thought in mind. Let me continue with the idea that she walked back here...it would have been a walk of about two miles, so it wouldn't have taken her long to arrive back here. I figure that she had a reason to further lure Deputy Sours into her little scheme; and being at the trailer, alone, in the dark of night would have made Sours a bit more vulnerable..."

"Interrupt me, Delmar, if you have a different opinion or if you think I'm not making sense," Lenny turned to Delmar and waited for his response.

"No, so far I agree totally with all you have put together. I don't have any different opinions to explain the course pf events," Delmar answered.

"So, then," Lenny continued, "she waited here for Deputy Sours—if that was actually him—and once the black pick-up arrived they hooked the pick-up to the trailer. Now, let's walk up here—not far now according to the GPS readings—where they turned the trailer around."

A short distance up the road, they came to a rough logging road that branched-off of the Forest road. Lanny checked his GPS coordinates and was convinced that they were just yards from the place where the bear carcass was found.

"This has to be the spot," Lenny shouted to Delmar who was a few yards behind. "Let me check my GPS once more; we will stop exactly at the place where my coordinates match those of the Forestry Department."

A few feet further and Lenny stated, "this is it. Let's examine this spot carefully...see if there is anything remaining of the bear carcass."

As they carefully searched the area, pushing aside vegetation and pieces of slag timber, Delmar asked Lenny to take a look at a clump of hair that was clinging to a piece of decaying tree branch.

"Good work, Delmar." Lanny agreed that it was indeed a piece of hair and that it had to be hair from the bear carcass. "We'll put that in an evidence bag; have a DNA assessment so that we can further prove that the bear carcass now in the possession of the Forestry boys is DNA-related to the hair we have found today."

"The issue now," Lenny began, "is to decide how to begin our search for the bullet and the skull. I do recall that Constance Meaning, the attorney representing Irana Dubliski, stated--during the meeting that we held to review all of the available evidence—that she had searched this area with a metal detector and had not found a bullet. So, we will scour this area once more and then search in a concentric method. If a predator, such as a coyote, was able to remove the skull from the carcass, we may have an impossible job trying to locate the skull and an even more difficult task trying to locate a bullet, especially if the bullet is still in the skull."

For nearly two hours the pair moved further and further from the site where the bear carcass had lain. Searching the area was made difficult by the presence of brush, last year's vegetation—now clumped and dead--and chunks and pieces of aging timber slag. Thus far, their search had yielded no success. As they moved upward onto a small rise, they encountered exposed rocks and large boulders, making their search more difficult.

Several more hours elapsed as they searched throughout the rocky terrain. They had climbed several hundred feet up the small hill above the site of the carcass. Lenny paused and shouted at Delmar, "Hey, let's go back and have lunch...I'm hungry. After we eat we can come back up here and search until it gets too dark."

Back at their vehicles they quickly devoured their lunch and critiqued their search efforts. Deciding that they had amply covered the area below the site of the carcass and, with willows and brush being so dense, they were unable to extend the search below the site. Hopefully, they thought, if a predator had removed the skull it would not have entered the willows and brush. Their decision was to continue the search among the rocks and boulders, where, they thought, a predator would be more apt to drag or carry the skull.

A quick look to the west warned them that good day light would soon be ebbing. Once more back in the rocky and boulder strewn area their search continued. It was not long before Delmar called to Lenny: "Come over here, Lenny, I think I have found something…don't know exactly because it is partially buried…all I can see is something that looks like a piece of bone…"

When Lenny stood next to Delmar, who was pointing to a place below a jagged boulder, he agreed with Delmar that he indeed had found something. "By golly," he stated, "that's more than we have found all day. Let's remove some of the dirt from around it and see if we can start to determine what it might be. We don't want to bump or thump it if we can help it…try to get the piece out of the ground intact."

On hands and knees they began to remove the earth from around the object. Soon, the curved crown of what appeared to be a skull was cleared of dirt. More digging around the object revealed jaw bones that were attached to the skull. Finally, the skull was totally unearthed. Gently handling the skull, Lenny carefully brushed away remaining dirt, and there in his hands was the object of their search: the bear's skull. Turning the skull for further examination, Lenny noted a small hole located at the rear of the skull, slightly below the apex or top of the skull. "Well, here is the bullet hole… at least it appears to be a bullet hole. And here is a small tuft of hair or fur. I'll tell you what I am gonna do…come Monday I am going to personally deliver this skull to the crime lab in Cheyenne. I am gonna ask for a DNA analysis of the skull…what we want is a DNA match with the bear carcass in the Forestry Department. I am also going to ask that the lab folks do what they can to determine if a bullet remains in the skull."

Lenny placed the skull into an evidence bag that he had carried with him. Once the skull was secured, the pair again used their metal detectors to search the possible path that a predator may have used to carry or drag the skull. They then concentrated on the immediate area where the skull had been found. They found nothing.

With the sun now dipping further on its westward journey, darkness would soon follow. It was time to return to their vehicles. Once there, Lenny summed up their achievements: "…Good day, Delmar, we have found the hair at the site where the carcass was first found; we have found the skull of that bear; and maybe, just maybe, the bullet is still in the skull. All in all some very valuable evidence that should prove to be interesting to a jury. Step by step we will have everything properly recorded and with good chain of evidence. What will really be of value will be the DNA analysis that will make it difficult for a defense attorney to attempt to disprove the importance of the bear carcass and the existence of the skull. We can't forget that, in theory, Irana Dubliski trained the bear to kill her husband, and then killed the bear so as to conceal her own acts as the perpetrator of a murder. At about this point she was becoming a bit careless. We just need to continue following the tracks that she left." Before leaving the area, Lenny advised Delmar that probably on Tuesday, after he had returned from Cheyenne, he would begin the examination of the trailer used by the Dubliskis. Wanting to know if Delmar would be available, Delmar told him that he had put in his notice at work for a two week vacation. They decided to meet in Rawlins on Tuesday at the County impound area where the trailer was being held. A good flashlight, Lenny advised, would be necessary.

CHAPTER EIGHT
SEARCHING THE TRAILER

As Delmar drove his Ford Bronco into the drive way to his cabin he saw Rhonda with a broom in her hands sweeping the deck. "We need some fire wood cut," she called to him as he stepped from his vehicle. He well understood that his work at his job and the time he was spending with Lanny were beginning to leave a number of his duties at his home neglected and in need of attention.

"I'll get the wood pronto," Delmar answered. To test her patience with him, he added, "we had a great day. We found some additional evidence; and, just before we gave up the search, we found the skull."

"I'm glad you had such a nice day," Rhonda answered somewhat sarcastically, I've been busy here doing housework and our laundry."

Delmar walked to his storage shed, found his axe, and began cutting fire wood. Later that evening, while sitting at the dinner table, Delmar told Rhonda that he had arranged to take the next two weeks as vacation time. His announcement that he would be going to Rawlins on Tuesday to assist Lanny inspect the trailer was met with Rhonda's raised eyes and silence.

"Why don't you come with me? You can do some shopping or visit some of our friends. It won't take long for Lenny and me to look over the trailer. Then, if you want, we can have lunch." Delmar hoped that his offer would bring him back into Rhonda's good graces.

"Hmm…I guess I can go along with that," Rhonda answered. "I need to spend some time at the library. Yeah, lunch sounds good."

While Delmar and Rhonda enjoyed the evening sitting before their fire place, Deputy Lenny Craig was busy at his home preparing his report that would explain the evidence found and the manner in which the search was conducted. As well, he wrote detailed suggestions—to be given to the crime lab in Cheyenne—for the examination of the skull, with emphasis placed on the possibility of a bullet being in the skull.

On Monday, the day after the skull had been found, Deputy Craig was on his way to Cheyenne. For Delmar, Monday would be a day to catch-up on the many projects that built-up throughout the long winter.

When Tuesday finally arrived, Delmar and Rhonda were in the Bronco on their way to Rawlins. It was always an enjoyable drive, especially during spring time. Passing through spring willow growth along the highway... driving through the narrows where the road became a small passage between a swampy area and rocky terrain...then through Elk Hollow... and finally through Saratoga and on to the interstate highway: the Bronco sped along its way.

Deputy Craig, meanwhile, had left his home in Encampment and had arrived at the Sheriff's office in Rawlins. There, he had made arrangements for another deputy to meet him and Delmar at the impound building. Deputy Craig had decided to "dust" the trailer for finger prints, as a means to establish that Irana Dubliski had been in contact with and had used the trailer.

Once in Rawlins, Delmar was dropped-off at the impound area; Rhonda was on her way to the library. Deputy Craig had arrived just moments before Delmar and was in the process of opening the door to the building where the trailer was stored.

"Hello, Delmar," Lenny called as Delmar approached the building. "I've been giving some thought to how we should examine the trailer," he paused, "...we need to prove that the trailer was involved in... even a critical element... in the murder. We can begin by taking some finger prints from the door and the door handle area. Let's do that first so we don't contaminate the area with our own prints. I would also like to obtain some identifying info, such as serial numbers and license plate number, to prove that the Dubliski's had either rented or purchased the trailer. And that brings to mind that the owner of the trailer, the fellow with the old circus, has tracked down the trailer and he says that the trailer belongs to him...he wants the trailer returned to him. So, we don't have long to inspect and obtain what we need from the trailer. Anyway, once we get the identifying info we can begin the search of the interior of the trailer."

"Sounds like a plan to me," Delmar chimed in. "I've got a good flashlight and I'm ready to go."

Once finger prints were obtained, Deputy Craig and Delmar entered the building. It was a one axel trailer; white exterior paneling; with mud spatters on the lower edge of the trailer. At the rear of the trailer the door consisted of two parts—with the two door parts opening in opposite directions.

Deputy Craig had written down the license plate number and was looking for a manufacturer's identification plate. "We're probably going to need to crawl under the trailer and get the numbers that will be on the axel."

"I guess I can do that," Delmar volunteered as he knelt beside and then crawled beneath the trailer.

"Ah ha," he mumbled, "here are the numbers. I'll try to get them written down." Once out from under the trailer he gave the paper containing the numbers to Lenny.

"Okay, let's go inside...see what we can find," Lenny directed.

Entering the trailer, flashlights luminating the interior of the trailer, they began their work. At the rear of the trailer Lenny found a large mass of hair or fur. "This will prove that the trailer was used to transport a bear. We'll keep the crime lab boys busy," Lenny smiled.

Along both sides of the trailer's interior were wooden slats affixed to upright supports. This structure began at floor level and continued upward for about five feet: a space or opening of about six inches existed between the slat structures and the wall of the trailer. With flashlights they peered into the opening.

Near the end of the trailer, at the door, Delmar asked Lenny to take a look at the bottom of the structure. "There is something down there," Delmar advised. "Can't tell for certain what it is...but it appears to be a metal object."

As Deputy Craig looked into the space he abruptly stated, "a metal object it is, and I bet that object is a pistol. We need to remove these lower slats so we can get at it. I'll have to go and get a battery powered hand drill so we can remove the screws that hold the slats against the supports. You stay here...don't allow anyone to enter this building."

Lenny left the area and drove to the Sheriff's office to obtain the drill. After about ten minutes he returned with the drill. Kneeling on the floor of the trailer, next to the lower slats, Lenny began removing the retaining screws. Soon the two lower slats had been removed.

"Well, well, look what we have here," Lenny exclaimed when he saw the object, "we have found a pistol…looks like a .38 caliber. If everything comes together like I think it will, …and if we find the bullet…ballistics will prove that this pistol was used to kill the bear. I can see Irana Dubliski now. She has just killed the bear. She walked back to the trailer and tossed this pistol into this open space, thinking that no one would ever find it. If I am correct, her finger prints will be all over this gun."

Lenny used a pen that he carried in his shirt pocket to retrieve the pistol. Placing the tube of the pen into the barrel of the pistol he gently raised the pistol upward from the floor. Then, he placed the weapon into an evidence container. "I'm ready to get this piece over to the crime lab," he stated.

"First," he added, "I think it would be a good idea to remove some of the dried mud from the side of the trainer, and also take a sample from beneath the trailer. Next time we are up where the bear carcass was found, we will collect some samples from the road. Eventual analysis should demonstrate that the trailer was on that Forestry road."

"Anything else we should do while we are here, Delmar?" Lenny asked.

"No, I believe we have covered all the bases. The evidence we have collected here will prove very damaging to the Dubliski woman once introduced during court proceedings," Delmar answered.

"Next stop, Delmar," Lenny began, "is to look into Clem Sours' death. I'll give you a call when I return from Cheyenne. Don't know that we will find anything, but it's worth a try."

They walked from the impound building, closed and locked the door, and stood for a moment to plan their next phase of the investigation. Lenny, looking toward the street, saw Rhonda waiting in the Ford Bronco. "Best hurry," Lenny said. "Don't want to keep your better-half waiting. Okay, my friend, I'll get this pistol and the hair over to the crime lab tomorrow. Maybe this afternoon I'll take a run up to the Forestry road and get a few samples of the dirt and mud on the road. I'll be back Thursday and, if you are able, we can meet Friday to sort through everything that is available that belonged to Clem Sours. I want to examine all of his personal items and I want to take a good look at his pick-up."

"Sounds fine to me," Delmar answered. "I have a bunch of chores to do around my place, so that will keep me busy. Where do you want to meet on Friday?"

"All of Sours' personal items are stored at the Sheriff's department. His pick-up has been stored in a special impound location. So, guess we will need to meet at the Sheriff's office," Lenny concluded.

They then parted ways: Deputy Craig returning to the Sheriff's office, and Delmar and Rhonda driving back to their home at Ryan Park.

"Did you find what you needed at the library?" Delmar asked Rhonda as they sped along the interstate highway.

"Oh, yeah," Rhonda responded. "I was looking for some new ideas for our meals…I thought that I might try to try some new dishes. So, you can look forward to several really spicy meals…that is if you are ever home long enough to even eat…"

Delmar well understood the message she had just sent. He knew that he needed to be more accommodating as he planned his time away with Lenny.

That afternoon and most of the next day Delmar cut fire wood, cleaned-up winter debris around his property, and applied a protective coat of varnish to the logs of his cabin. At supper on Thursday evening Delmar cautiously told Rhonda that he would be making a trip back to Rawlins to meet with Lenny. His offer for Rhonda to accompany him was accepted. A good time to shop and maybe back to the library, she said.

CHAPTER NINE

FRIDAY: DEPUTY CLEM SOURS AND A REVIEW OF HIS DEATH

Friday finally arrived and Delmar and Rhonda were again traveling the familiar route to Rawlins. Once there Rhonda left Delmar at the Sheriff's office, and she went on her way to attend to her interests. Inside the office Delmar met Deputy Craig who had just left a meeting with the Sheriff. "I just gave the Sheriff a progress report," Lenny said, "I think that he was pretty impressed with what we have so far found. He had a few questions about the bear's skull and the pistol. Otherwise, he is looking forward to my full report. Let's head down to the storage area and begin going through Sours' property.

On a long table, near the middle of the room, they placed all of Sours' property. Items to examine were: clothing, shoes and boots, a wallet, note books, the coroner's report describing Sours' death, photos of Sours sitting in his pick-up—photos taken when Sours was found--documents retrieved from official computers used by Sours when he was first attempting to obtain information about the Dubliskis, and Sours' service pistol. It would be a long and tedious task to examine all of the items. When finished they would examine Sours' pick-up.

Each item, beginning with the clothing, was carefully examined. No clues as to Sours' involvement with Irana Dubliski were discovered. As the boots were examined Lenny noticed dried mud located at the heel and on several other places. "I'll scrape some of this mud into an evidence container. If it matches the mud and dirt on that Forestry road, we can definitely place Sours on the road up there," Lenny concluded.

When reading the note books that Sours had carried with him, they learned that Sours had discovered that both Irana and Georgio Dubliski were fugitives from Russia where Gregorio Dubliski was wanted for the murder of a Russian police officer. Irana Dubliski, Sours' notes revealed, was illegally in the United States. Computer documents revealed that Sours had discovered that the Dubliskis had been living in a down-and-out circus in Pontiac, Michigan. The owner of the failing circus, according to Sours' search, stated that the Dubliskis had stolen a trailer and a trained bear. A rental company reported that Georgio Dubliski had rented a 1980 Lincoln, green in color.

Why Clem Sours had not reported this information to his superiors became evident when, in Sours' personal diary, a written entry described the attraction that Sours had formed for Irana Dubliski. He was protecting her, Lenny thought; however, Irana Dubliski, aware of what Sours had learned about them, was fearful that Sours would eventually report them. Were Sours to report them, deportation would result. Irana Dubliski, Lenny was convinced, had a motive for murder. "And I believe that we have collected the necessary evidence to prove that assumption," Lenny concluded.

Before leaving the Sheriff's office they returned all of the Sours' items to the assigned storage space. Lenny, after properly "signing-out" for the Sours' service revolver, carried the weapon upstairs to the finger print lab for a second check for finger prints.

"I guess now's the time to head over to take a look at Sours' pick-up. It shouldn't take long because the pick-up has been given a fine-toothed-comb examination just after it was found. Maybe we can figure out a different angle for our search," Lenny spoke more to himself than to Delmar.

A quick drive to the impound area and they were standing at the rear of the black pick-up. After a few quick photographs of the pick-up, Lenny commented, "…no one has been in or around the pick-up since the lab boys finished their examination and search…anyway let's take a look around."

They began with a look into the interior of the truck, taking photographs of the window on the left side of the cab. The window contained the exit hole of the bullet that had passed through Clem Sours' brain. Blood spatters were readily apparent over much of the window's surface. "It's hard for me to imagine that Sours sat here in this seat, behind the steering wheel, and placed his revolver to his right temple and pulled the trigger. If he actually intended to kill himself, why didn't he leave the pick-up and do the act outside the pick-up? Nope, just doesn't make sense. Sours was attracted to the Dubliski woman. He was probably riding on a happy cloud as he thought of his chances of being with this woman. He wasn't depressed—he was over-joyed with the attention she was giving him. He had no reason to kill himself." Lenny ended his soliloquy and turned to Delmar who was looking beneath the seats of the vehicle, "Delmar," he asked, "who do you suppose was in this pick-up sitting right next to him?"

"It doesn't take much effort to answer that.," Delmar answered. "The person sitting next to him was none other than Irana Dubliski. I would bet that Sours had pulled the trailer back to the place where the Dubliskis were staying, and there he helped her hook the trailer to her car. She was probably on her way to other parts, but before she left she had to take care of Sours. Somehow, she convinced Sours to drive her to that isolated place where the pick-up was eventually found, perhaps luring him with a romantic nudge or two. Once the pick-up was parked she waited for the proper time. Most likely she found that his service revolver was right there, even lying on the seat between them. She took the pistol, gently raised it to his head...he probably didn't even feel the barrel of the gun...and pulled the trigger. Then, she wiped the interior of the pick-up clean, erasing her finger prints. Also, she wiped the gun clean and placed it in Sours' limp right hand. She then left the pick-up and walked to her vehicle and drove away from the Ryan Park area. There are several gaps that need to be filled in, but I believe I am pretty close to correctly describing the events surrounding Sours' death."

"You have most likely and very correctly described the scenario," Lenny agreed. "We don't know where the Dubliski woman had left her vehicle while she was with Sours, and we can only surmise that she walked back to her car, which was probably not far from where she killed Sours. Anyway, she left Carbon County and was later arrested in Omaha. Okay, let's get back to looking over the pick-up."

Again, Delmar knelt down to look beneath the seats while Lenny examined the storage areas in the Pick-up. "Hmmm, what's this?" Delmar mumbled. "Looks like a piece of tissue paper or a Kleenex."

"Don't touch it, Delmar," Lanny warned. "It could be something that the woman left, and it could contain the DNA prints of the owner. If it does yield Dubliski's DNA we can't prove that she left it at the time of the murder but it will be enough to prove that she had been in the pick-up at some time." The tissue paper was carefully removed and placed in an evidence container. Lenny recorded the time, date, and place of recovery.

As they slowly walked around the pick-up they noticed mud splatters on fenders and hub caps. "I'll take some samples of this dried mud; have it analyzed; and hope it matches the samples of the mud and dirt collected from the Forestry road. If the results show a positive correlation between the dried mud on the pick-up and the mud from the Forestry road we will have additional proof that the pick-up was on the Forestry road near the site of the murder and the site where the bear carcass was found," Lenny counseled.

"Not much left for us here," Lenny advised. "We didn't find much, but if that tissue paper and the mud splatters prove positive we will have made a big leap in this investigation. I will transport this evidence over to the crime lab—they will tire of me pretty soon. Now, Delmar, we have to patiently wait for the crime lab to complete the analysis of the skull and other samples that we have given them. We're probably looking at a four to six weeks wait for the results."

With the examination of Sours' belongings and his pick-up completed, Delmar waited on a bench outside the Sheriff's department for Rhonda's return. Soon she pulled up at the curb and Delmar and Rhonda were on their way to Ryan park.

Delmar finished his vacation and continued working at his chores around his home and property. Discussions about the investigation ebbed and only occasionally surfaced during daily conversations. Delmar, feeling that the tension between he and Rhonda was easing, did not press his luck by broaching the subject any more than necessary. He well understood that she disapproved of his involvement in the investigation, and he knew that her displeasure would again arise once Lenny received the crime lab reports, at which time he may be called to assist Lenny.

Four weeks, then six, and at the end of the eighth week Delmar received a telephone call from Lenny who told him that the crime lab results were sitting on the Sheriff's desk. "I haven't read the entire report, but what I have read looks good," Lenny advised. "Come over when you can and we will review the reports."

Delmar was now back at his place of employment and it would be the weekend before he was able to meet Lenny in Rawlins.

CHAPTER TEN
A REVIEW OF THE EVIDENCE

Throughout the eight weeks lull in the investigation, Delmar had remained active at his place of employment and many projects around his home and property had been completed. It was now into August and Delmar's thoughts had turned to the necessary preparations for the upcoming winter. Looking back, he found it difficult to believe how he had waited for spring to arrive and for the investigation to begin. Now, winter was not far away; but new phases in the investigation of Irana Dubliski were on the agenda.

Saturday arrived and Delmar and Rhonda were on their way to Rawlins to meet Deputy Lenny Craig. It was late morning when they arrived at the Sheriff's office. Rhonda left Delmar at the office and she drove to the library. Upon entering the office, Delmar found Deputy Craig in the conference room arranging the documents and boxes that the crime lab had produced.

"Mornin', Delmar," Lenny greeted Delmar as he stepped into the room. "The crime lab," he began, "has finished-up their work...maybe they have one or two additional items to inspect and test...otherwise they have given us some fine results. What we need to do today is to organize the documents and then begin to place our assumptions and conclusions in written form. I have met with Dan Lassiter, the County Attorney, and he wants us to deliver the evidence and any conclusions regarding the murder that we may have. He would like this information as soon as we can put it all together. Once he has the information he will make a decision regarding the arrest of Irana Dubliski. In my opinion, we have sufficient evidence to warrant the arrest of that woman...but we will see..."

Several boxes and file holders were arranged on a table. The first box that Lenny opened contained the skull of the bear, and as he removed the skull he handed the skull to Delmar, and with a smile, he said, "you will be surprised, Delmar. The crime lab removed a .38 caliber slug from the skull; and, just as important, ballistics results indicate that the slug was fired by the pistol that we found in the trailer. Guess whose finger prints were on the pistol? Certainly! The prints belonged to Irana Dubliski."

A second box contained the soil samples taken from the trailer and from Sours' pick-up, while a third box contained the soil samples collected from the Forestry road. The lab reports indicate that the samples taken from the trailer and pick-up and the Forestry road were one and the same. The final box contained the hair and fur samples removed from the bear carcass as well as the hair and fur samples collected at the site where the carcass had been found. Samples of hair remaining on the skull and the fur found in the trailer had also been analyzed by the crime lab. The report submitted by the lab indicated that all the samples had but one source: the bear carcass.

Finally, a small envelope—consisting of the tissue paper that Delmar had found beneath the passenger seat in Deputy Sours' pick-up—contained DNA results that matched Irana Dubliski's DNA sample taken during her arrest nearly a year ago.

Within the file holders were the crime lab's report describing the manner in which the evidence was received, the tests conducted, the manner in which the tests were completed, and the results of the tests. The report also included the name of each person who conducted the tests, as well as the training, experience and professional back-ground of each person.

"Well, Delmar, it would appear that we have done our work," Lenny said as he began returning evidence and written documents back to their proper boxes and file holders. "Now," Lenny continued, "I need to complete a narrative of our suspicions and conclusions. Let me just mention what I plan to place in the narrative. I will begin with your discovery of the body; mention the Coroner's examination and Dr. Purdy's report; discuss why we believe that Irana Dubliski trained the bear that undoubtedly shoved the arrow in the victim; and describe the search that you and I made when we found the arrow and the pieces of burlap." Lenny thought for a moment and continued: "...oh yes, I will include the statements of the witness--who have provided affidavits—who will testify that they saw the vehicle traffic that night, with emphasis on the trailer being pulled in and out of Ryan Park. Along with that I will discuss our assumptions about Irana Dubliski's movement of the trailer, her return to the place she was staying, and our belief that she summoned Deputy Sours for his help. I will also inform the County Attorney of the proof we have that Sours' pick-up was on the Forestry road and was used to pull the trailer—the proof, of course, being the soil samples and the witness statements. When the County Attorney and his staff examine the evidence we collected and the crime lab reports they will be able to connect the evidence to a variety of conclusions. Anything else that I should put in the report, Delmar?"

"The death of Clem Sours is a huge issue," Delmar began. "Perhaps your report should include our beliefs that Sours was infatuated with the Dubliski woman. Those beliefs, of course, based on the notes that Sours had written in his diary. Maybe the County Attorney will agree that Sours was not a depressed person bent on killing himself, but a person excited by the attention that the Dubliski woman was offering. The County Attorney can do a lot with that tissue paper containing Dubliski's DNA. Anyway, we need to emphasize that we do not believe Sours' death was a suicide. Remember, that Irana Dubliski had a motive for killing Sours: she was fearful that he would eventually report what he had discovered about her and her husband. Frankly, I am hoping that she will be found guilty of murdering Clem Sours."

"Good idea...yes, I was going to add our assumptions about Sours' activities with the Dubliski woman, especially his involvement with her the night that her husband was killed by the bear. Speaking of the bear...I will add our assumptions that she trained the bear to kill her husband. Anything else?" Lenny asked.

"Okay, I found the body on May 1...a year ago. It well appears that the victim was killed the night before. Just mentioning that in case the County Attorney needs a time-line as a beginning. You already have that info in your records, so no big deal. Hmmm..." Delmar thought, "...guess we could add a comment or two about the bear carcass and that metal cuff on the bear's leg...just to let the County Attorney understand how the bear delivered the arrow. What about a comment or two about our suspicions that she killed and concealed the bear to cover the issue of the bear being trained? The County Attorney, of course--using the bear skull, the slug found in the skull, and the pistol we found in the trailer—will easily tie the woman to the death of the bear. Other than those issues you have given the County Attorney concrete evidence that should help him to convict Irana Dubliski."

Lenny thought for a moment and stated, "...As I begin writing the narrative I should be able to organize all of this, placing the events and our conclusions in good order. I do agree with you that we should push hard for a conviction for the death of Sours. Dubliski's husband was a drunk and an abusive person, so society did not lose much when he was put down; but, Clem Sours was a law enforcement officer and he deserves more than being written-off as a suicide. Know what I intend to do?" Lenny asked with a glint in an upraised eye, "I am going to go and meet with Dr. Purdy. I will tell him what we have learned, especially about Sours probably being attracted to the Dubliski woman and being enamored by the attention she was giving him. I'll try to convince him that Sours had no reason to kill himself. He wasn't depressed or despondent: he was enjoying the possibility that he might become involved with this woman. If Dr. Purdy will change the death certificate to even read "possible homicide," we will have a chance of obtaining a conviction for first degree murder."

"Great idea, Lenny," Delmar joined in. "I wonder if you should take Sours' diary with you so Dr. Purdy can read Sours' comments about the woman?"

"I'll do just that," Lenny answered. "After I meet with Dr. Purdy I'll give you a call," Lenny advised.

After returning to Ryan Park it was work as usual for Delmar. Although busy at his place of employment and with his chores around his home, time seemed to slowly elapse. Delmar waited for Lenny's call, hoping to hear something positive from Dr. Purdy.

CHAPTER ELEVEN
DR. PURDY

After concluding the review of the crime lab reports with Delmar, Lenny immediately drove to the funeral home where Dr. Purdy had his office. Once in the building, Lenny removed his hat, and seated himself in a waiting room. It was not long before an attendant greeted Lenny and asked him his purpose. Lenny told the attendant that he would appreciate being able to have a word with Dr. Purdy. The attendant left and soon reappeared to advise Lenny that Dr. Purdy would meet with him. Lenny was escorted to Dr. Purdy's office.

"Come in, come in," Dr. Purdy's friendly voice greeted Lenny. "I know you…you're Deputy Craig. Met you at the Sours' inquest. What can I do for you?" Dr. Purdy was a pudgy man; friendly round face that most often contained a cigar; thick lensed glasses rested on his nose; and a head that once contained ample hair.

"Thank you for being able to meet with you. I am here to share some information that I have discovered about Clem Sours. Thought you might want to hear about what I have learned." Lenny paused and waited for Dr. Purdy's invitation to continue.

"Go ahead…I've got some time," Dr. Purdy urged as he tapped ashes from a cigar stub.

"To begin, Sours was somehow involved with the wife of the murder victim, Gregorio Dubliski. I believe that Sours had discovered that the Dubliskis were illegally in the United States after fleeing Russia where Gregorio had killed a police officer. Irana Drubliski, the wife, began to believe that Sours had discovered very incriminating evidence about her and her husband. She most likely flouted her good looks and offered a few hints that she would appreciate Sours' company. Soon, I believe, she lured

Sours into agreeing to help her and to assist her—beginning with borrowing money from Sours and accepting his offer to purchase gasoline for her car."

Lenny paused to "read" Dr. Purdy's interest and attention level. Dr. Purdy sat at his desk, his white lab coat covering most of his large frame, cigar stub in hand...clearly listening to Lenny.

"To make a long story short," Lenny continued, "I have evidence that Sours appeared in Ryan Park—probably about 11 P.M.—on the night of the murder of Gregorio Dubliski. He was seen driving into Ryan Park and later he was seen pulling a trailer on his way out of Ryan Park. Let me clarify. His pick-up was seen, and soil samples taken from his pick-up established that he had been on the Forestry road just below where the murder victim' body was found. It is interesting that witnesses saw a car pulling a trailer into Ryan Park, and later they saw the car leaving Ryan Park without the trailer. Then, the pick-up appeared; entered Ryan Park; and not long after left Ryan Park pulling a trailer."

Lenny explained the theory that Irana Dubliski had pulled the trailer to the Forestry road; unloaded a trained bear that would place an arrow in her husband's back; loaded the bear back into the trailer; unhooked the car from the trailer; drove her car to the cabin where she had been staying; probably called Sours while at the cabin; walked back to the trailer and waited for Sours.

"So, what are you getting at?" Dr. Purdy interrupted.

"I believe," Lenny continued, "that Irana Dubliski lured Clem Sours into a plot that specifically consisted of killing him. Her motive was to eliminate Sours before he had the chance to report her and her husband to his superiors. She lured him to Ryan Park that night in order to find a way to be alone with him. Here..." Lanny offered, "...is Sours' personal diary. This particular entry describes Sours' attraction to Irana Dubliski."

Dr. Purdy accepted the diary and read the entry. Taking a long puff on the cigar stub, he commented, "very interesting. What more do you have?"

The diary was returned to Lenny and he continued his discourse. "The murder of Gregorio Dubliski most likely occurred on the evening before May 1, 1982. Clem Sours, according to your autopsy report, probably met his death on or just before May 1, 1982. I believe that Irana Dubliski killed her husband the evening before May 1. She was with Clem Sours just hours after her husband was killed, and I believe that same night or early the next morning, she was sitting with Sours in his pick-up. Finally,

Dr. Purdy, it is impossible for me to believe that Sours was depressed or otherwise in a funk that would have moved him to suicide. He was most likely elated and excited that Irana was paying attention to him. In other words, he had no reason to kill himself. He had every reason to be patient and wait for the proper time to share his feelings with her."

"Keep going; I'm listening," Dr. Purdy interrupted, now taking notes on a pad on his desk.

"Not much more," Lenny answered. "I believe that she convinced Sours to drive to the spot where his pick-up was eventually found. There, she found Sours' service pistol…at least that is my suspicion…lying on the seat next to Sours. She took the pistol and carefully placed it next to his right temple and pulled the trigger. She wiped the interior of the pick-up clean of her prints and cleaned the pistol of her prints. She walked back to her car, and the next we know of her she is in Omaha, Nebraska. That's it. I do believe, however, that the murder of Gregorio Dubliski and Clem Sours' death occurred in such close time-frame that mere coincidence cannot be a factor. We have ample evidence to prove that the Dubliski woman killed her husband; and, based on evidence we have thus far collected, we are certain that she was with Clem Sours the night of his death. That's it, Dr. Purdy. Hope it makes sense…"

"Listen to me, young man," Dr. Purdy began, "I do not often find reason to change any decisions I make regarding the cause of death; but, after listening to your information, I will compare that which you have just told me with the report that your office provided after finding Clem Sours' body. I do not often make mistakes, but perhaps it is possible that I was given insufficient information just before the autopsy. I expect to be able to read all reports that may be in the County Attorney's possession."

"Thank you, Dr. Purdy. I appreciate the time you have allowed." Lenny offered his hand to Dr. Purdy for a farewell gesture. Dr. Purdy accepted the hand-shake.

"I'll certainly let you know of my decision. I have some work to do before I can actually render a decision." Dr. Purdy extinguished the cigar stub in an ash tray as an appropriate way to end the meeting.

─── CHAPTER TWELVE ───
THE COUNTY ATTORNEY'S OFFICE

Four weeks had passed since Deputy Craig's meeting with Dr. Purdy. It was now near the last week of September, and such things as hunting season and preparations for winter were sure to interfere with the investigation. The County Attorney's office, however, was not to be distracted. Once Dan Lassiter and his staff had completed their review of the evidence provided by Lenny and the Sheriff's department, Dan summoned Lenny to his office.

"Here, Lenny, have a cup of coffee," Dan greeted Lenny once Lenny was seated in the conference room." Lenny admired Dan's expensive alligator boots, and his dark, western-style suit. On the table rested Dan's Stetson white hat. Dan, about 50 years old, was a handsome, youthful appearing man. Grey hair and signs of age had yet to visit Dan. Around the courthouse it was a common belief that Dan's good looks swayed jury members more than did his orations.

"The information that you submitted to my office, Lenny, will make my job much easier as we get into this case. I will tell you now that there seems to be enough evidence to issue an arrest warrant for Irana Dubliski…there are…" Dan paused, "…several issues that will give the defense attorney the opportunity to question and try to discredit our course of prosecution. For example, I need to work on a way to prove that woman trained the bear to kill her husband. The information that you have provided about her travels in and out of Ryan Park with the trailer will certainly help me make that connection. And, of great help will be the pistol, with her finger prints, that you found in the trailer."

At that moment, Dan's secretary entered the room to tell him that Judge Wolfe was on the telephone. "Okay," Dan said. "I best take this call."

In a few moments Dan returned to the conference room and, after looking at his note pad, stated, "now, where was I…oh, yes, the next issue is connecting her to Deputy Sours' death. The fact that her husband's death occurred just hours before Sours' death will give me some leverage; however, the big boost that I will have is Dr. Purdy's reversal of suicide as the cause of Sours' death. Dr. Purdy said that his reason for reversing the suicide conclusion was based on the information that you shared with him. I examined that information, Lenny, and it is very good. I think a jury will accept that reasoning as a credible and valid link to Sours' death. The information that you presented will aid me as I lay the ground-work to establish motive, premeditation, and even malice. All of these issues, of course, lead to a charge of first degree murder."

Dan took several moments to read through the notes he had made regarding the evidence. He resumed his comments. "Of course, there are one or two other areas that involve suspicion and conjecture, but court rules allow circumstantial evidence to a certain point. I will just have to lay good ground-work as I approach each of these issues. Now, I guess, is a good time to begin planning for the witness list. As we better prepare for a trial, this witness list and schedule may change. For now, though, this is what I plan: I will need Delmar Mentis as the first to testify, followed by Dr. Purdy; then I will need you, Lenny, and the witnesses who observed the movement of the trailer; and, most likely, I will need representatives from the crime lab. As I produce evidence, you and crime lab experts may be recalled to the witness stand several times. Well, that is about the gist of it. My staff and I have much work to accomplish before we can even begin thinking about a trial. I will give you the warrant for Irana Dubliski's arrest before you leave my office. Then, you people at the Sheriff's office need to plan your agenda for the return of the Dubliski woman, which may include extradition procedures when you locate her."

Deputy Craig received the arrest warrant and returned to the Sheriff's department. Once there the plans were laid for the arrest and return of Irana Dubliski to Carbon County.

CHAPTER THIRTEEN
THE ARREST OF NORA DOLOR

Lenny was now able to begin his journey to his home in Encampment, but first he needed to stop by the Sheriff's office and deliver the arrest warrant. At the office he found Sheriff Chester Overman speaking to one of the jailors. The Sheriff—a man of about 55 years, dressed in a white and blue western shirt, wearing faded Levis and well-worn western boots—tossed Lenny a wave to acknowledge his presence.

Lenny respected the Sheriff and enjoyed working for and with him. While the Sheriff looked far older than the 55 years or so—with greying hair and deeply etched lines of age—Lenny never doubted the man's capabilities. The Sheriff had spent much of his life as a ranch-hand, but fortune smiled on him when he became acquainted with several prominent men while guiding a hunting party. With support from those men Sheriff Overman found himself as a successful candidate for the position of sheriff—a position he had occupied for nearly ten years.

"What can I do for you, Lenny," the Sheriff asked once his conversation with the jailor had ended. "I suspect that paper you have in your hand is an arrest warrant. Dan Lassiter just told me he had issued the warrant."

"Yes, sir, Sheriff, we finally have a warrant for Irana Dubliski's arrest… and I'm ready to go find her," Lenny answered the Sheriff, well knowing that the Sheriff would not assign him to that task.

Smiling, the Sheriff met Lenny's attempt at a bit of humor with, "sorry, Lenny, you know that I have to assign two deputies who have been totally neutral in this investigation. So, I will assign a female and a male to try to find that woman. This being Friday, I will try to have them on the road Monday. Before they leave I will notify the authorities in Omaha of the warrant, and ask them to maybe give us a hand in locating the woman."

"Any help that law enforcement in Omaha can give us will make our job easier," Lenny answered. "Now that you have the warrant I think I will be on my way home. With all of the time Delmar and I have spent on this investigation my wife, Kathy, probably considers me as a stranger. So, Sheriff, you have a good weekend…if you need me for anything, just holler."

"Get out of here…better rest-up because if that woman is returned to us things will get busy." The Sheriff took Lenny's arm and escorted him to the door.

Two deputies, Amy Wright and Ed Donley, were assigned to travel to Omaha, locate Irana Dubliski, arrest her, and return her to Carbon County. Their assignment would prove to be anything but a routine arrest.

When Monday arrived, Sheriff Overman met with the two deputies and offered his suggestions as how to locate Irana Dubliski. After giving the deputies the last known address for Irana, he suggested that they first make contact with Omaha authorities. Letting the authorities know that they were in the community and describing their purpose would be crucial the Sheriff instructed.

On their way to Omaha the deputies discussed their strategy for locating Irana Dubliski. Contacting the police and sheriff authorities would be their first official duties, followed by finding a suitable motel. As they neared Omaha traffic became heavier and their conversation turned to driving conditions and decisions for which exit to use to enter Omaha.

Once in the city they located the police department; introduced themselves; and explained their purpose. The deputies were assured of assistance and cooperation. Before leaving the office, the deputies were offered a tour of the city and an invitation to have dinner later in the evening. Next, a visit to the sheriff's department resulted in similar greetings. A detective at the sheriff's office drove the two deputies to the address previously given by Irana Dubliski. They would visit that address the next day.

A member of the police department arrived at the motel to drive the deputies to a restaurant for dinner. After an enjoyable evening the deputies returned to their motel rooms. Refreshed following a sound sleep, the deputies quickly downed breakfast and set-out to locate the Dubliski woman.

Their first stop was the address that the police department had shown them. There, it was an apartment building and an employee directed them to the apartment for which they were looking. A knock at the door was answered by an elderly woman who told them that she had been living in the apartment for nearly a year. She did not know Irana Dubliski and had never heard of her.

In such a large city with so many people, finding one specific person seemed an almost impossible task. They left the apartment building, and drove to a coffee shop where they discussed their options. Somewhere in the city, they believed, Irana Dubliski had to leave her "finger prints." But where? They drove to the police department, then to the sheriff's office; however, neither department had records of nor contacts with Irana Dubliski. A suggestion was made by a police detective that the office of vital statistics may possibly provide some information. The detective gave them directions to that office.

Soon, they were in the office of vital statistics where they explained their purpose to a clerk who, after examining their credentials, entered the name of Irana Dubliski into an office computer. She returned to the deputies and explained to them that a person named Irana Dubliski had applied for a change of name. Eventually, the clerk told them, Irana Dubliski's name had been changed to Nora Dolor. The clerk handed them a piece of paper that contained the name of Nora Dolor and the address given at the time of the name change.

At the address given by the clerk, the deputies quietly stepped to the door of the apartment. Amy on one side of the door while Ed stood before the door and gave a knock. No answer. Ed gave several louder knocks, but still no answer. The deputies decided that the woman was probably at her place of employment, and their only option was to move their vehicle in such a position so that they were able to observe all pedestrian traffic going in and out of the apartment building.

For several hours they waited. Finally, at about 5:30 P.M., they observed a small woman approaching the apartment building. "That's her," Amy nearly whispered, as if the woman would over hear them. "Let's go get her."

Irana Dubliski, or Nora Dolor as she now was known, saw the deputies cross the street toward her. They blocked her way into the building, and guided her into the wall of the building. "Nora Dolor?" Ed calmly asked.

"Yes, I am Nora Dolor." The woman answered. She knew that what she had for so long dreaded was now taking place. Eyes wide with fear, and struggling for breath, she managed to ask what they wanted.

"Nora Dolor, or Irana Dubliski, you are being arrested for the murder of your husband, Gregorio Dubliski, and for the murder of Sheriff Deputy Clem Sours," the deputy informed her. After the deputy read her the Miranda rights, he then informed her that she would be taken to the local sheriff's department, where she would spend the night. There, she was advised, she could decide whether she desired to participate in extradition proceedings.

At the sheriff's department in Omaha, Nora Dolor was "booked" as a hold-over for Wyoming. The next morning the two Wyoming Deputies arrived at the office and briefly interviewed Nora. They were told by the woman that she would waive her rights to extradition, preferring to return to Wyoming. The Omaha authorities consulted with their attorney who asked Nora Dolor to sign documents which indicated her approval to waive extradition. It was just a matter of minutes before she was released from custody. The Wyoming deputies thanked the Omaha authorities for their cordiality and assistance, and the group from Wyoming were on the road back to Carbon County.

Nora Dolor remained silent, not uttering a word, the entire trip back to Rawlins. Deep in thought, considering what options were left, she found herself virtually without direction as to what she might attempt. Deciding to merely remain silent and wait for a lawyer to be appointed, she thought, would be the best course of action. Then, she believed, when she had the opportunity to review the evidence, she would begin to organize some strategy that could possibly save her from the fate that she was dreading.

Arriving in Rawlins late that evening, the trio made their way to the county jail where Nora Dolor would spend several months before a trial would be scheduled. Nora was "booked-in," photographed, finger printed, and given a brief physical exam. Based on her overall demeanor— withdrawn and depressed—she was placed on a suicide watch. Before being placed in a cell she was told that probably the next day she would receive her initial court hearing.

That night as she lay on the uncomfortable jail mattress, she relived each element of the crimes which she had committed. In doing so she gave thought to the depth of the investigation that had now resulted in her arrest. Only credible, incriminating evidence would have led the county to a decision to arrest her. She decided that she would make no decisions until she was given the opportunity to meet with an attorney and be given her rights as a defendant to examine the evidence. Until then, she must wait with as much composure as possible.

Her sleep that night was fitful with only minutes of actual rest. As a precaution, meant to monitor her throughout the night, the lights in her cell remained on throughout the night, contributing further to her discomfort.

She was awake, sitting on the bed, when a female jailor came to her cell with a tray for breakfast. Nora refused the tray but accepted a cup of coffee. The jailer instructed her to prepare herself for her court appearance. Nora splashed water from the sink over her face and arranged her long hair as was possible without a comb or brush. Soon she was led from her cell and placed in hand restraints. She looked not at all like a person accused of a double homicide. In fact, her petite body-type and almost dainty physical features were in opposition to that which one would expect of a murderess. Dressed in orange jump-suit, much too large for her size, she appeared as a rather pathetic person.

Nora Dolor was dwarfed by the two deputies who escorted her to the circuit court where Judge Anders presided. At the direction of the clerk of court, the deputies and Nora Dolor entered the court room. Nora was told to sit at a table located in front of the Judge's position. In addition to the Judge, a clerk, and a court reporter was Deputy Lenny Craig.

An "ALL RISE" command--followed by a shuffle of chairs—was issued by the clerk when Judge Anders entered the court room. "Please be seated," the Judge addressed the group. When instructed to rise, Nora Dolor moved her chair back from the table and stood as instructed.

Nora Dolor was informed of the purpose of the hearing, basically a decision to decide if sufficient evidence warranted her case to be remanded to the District Court of Carbon County. Not a trial, the Judge informed Nora, only a hearing to examine the evidence.

Deputy Craig was called to the witness stand where he gave a summary of the investigation and the evidence thus far collected. Judge Anders then recessed the proceedings so that she could more extensively review the evidence provided by the County Attorney. Once that process was completed, the Judge called the court to order and informed Nora Dolor that she found sufficient reason to refer the case to the District Court.

During the District Court arraignment, Nora Dolor would be granted the right to enter a plea. Then, the court would "set" bail and appoint an attorney, if the defendant were unable to afford an attorney. Court was then adjourned and Nora Dolor was returned to her jail cell.

CHAPTER FOURTEEN
PRE-TRIAL PROCEEDINGS

NORA DOLOR

Deprived of beauty aids, Nora Dolor made the best of a bad situation. She was unable to apply the make-up that she daily used to maintain her appearance. Now, pale and appearing even haggard, she longed for the time when her looks were that of a much younger woman. Her concerns for her once good looks were all too soon replaced by the fears of what lay ahead. She had yet to be afforded the opportunity to examine the evidence that would be used in the pending trial; however, that issue would soon be resolved as today she would appear in District Court where she would be appointed an attorney.

With a loud clatter the barred door of her cell was opened and two deputies stood ready to escort her to District Court. "Hurry up," one of the deputies commanded, "we need to transport you to your court appearance." Hand restraints were applied, and, with Nora Dolor between the two deputies, they made their way to a waiting vehicle and on their way to the hearing. The hearing itself was much the same as the hearing she received in the circuit court; however, District Court was presided over by Judge James Wolfe. Bespectacled, bushy grey hair, a rather large person, and a well-respected man about Carbon County, Judge Wolfe had been briefly informed of the elements of the case before him. He sat for several moments gazing about the court room—assessing the identity of the people who were in his bailiwick today—and then he fixed his gaze upon Nora Dolor. What thoughts were in his mind one can only guess. Perhaps, in his best legal judgement, he summarized the situation as "… well, well what is to become of you, Nora Dolor?"

After calling several witnesses, in particular Lenny Craig and Delmar Mentis, Judge Wolfe politely asked Nora Dolor to stand and address the court with her plea of guilty or not guilty. Nora Dolor quickly stood and with a calm voice, but with obvious Russian accent, stated, "Your honor, I respectfully enter my plea of not guilty." "Very well," Judge Wolfe answered, "…your plea is accepted. You will be appointed an attorney and you will be held in custody without bail. This hearing is now concluded."

Several days following the District Court hearing Nora Dolor was visited by the attorney appointed by the court. Her first opportunity to meet her attorney was in an interview room where, upon entering the room, she met the man who was to become her attorney. "My name is David Grimley," the man said as he rose from his chair to greet Nora. She inspected David Grimley as one might evaluate a foe soon to be met in some type of conflict. David Grimley was a man of about 40 years. She noticed that he was beginning to lose his hair, and that his mid-section was the repository of many bottles of beer. He appeared somewhat disheveled in a brown suit, with a yellow tie that was not well centered at the neck of a white shirt. It had been probably three days since his last shave. She was correct in her assumption that he was a cigarette smoker as a pack of cigarettes was noticeable in his shirt pocket. Brown shoes, in need of polish, ended her first evaluation of this man who had been assigned to guide her through a process that may well result in the end of her life.

"Hello," Nora managed to say. "My name is Nora Dolor."

"We have a great deal to discuss today, Nora. First, I want you to understand that if you are not absolutely honest with me I cannot and will not attempt to defend you. I want you to know that I have had a brief conversation with Constance Meaning, your attorney of last…it is my impression that you were dishonest with her. That shall not occur between you and me. If you choose to be dishonest I will rapidly request that I be removed from your case. Understood?" David coldly challenged.

Nora sat in a chair near a table and looked upward at the ceiling. "How can I be honest with this person whom I have just met? How can I even answer that question when I know nothing about him? How do I know that he will value my truths and not betray me?' Those were the flood of first thoughts that entered her mind. Answering his question, she stated, "…yes, I understand." She said no more.

"Very well…I also understand that you need to become acquainted with me and we will hope that process will be able to develop as we go along. We will slowly move into the difficult aspects, that is the more in depth charges pending against you as we begin to feel more comfortable and trusting of one another. "So, Nora," David began as he attempted to gain her confidence, "tell me a little about yourself."

Nora remained silent for a few moments and then proceeded to relate how she had met Gregorio Dubliski and how they had managed to arrive in the United States after Gregorio had killed the Russian police officer. She began to embellish her description of life with Gregorio with examples of his abusive behavior and his use of alcohol. As she entered the phase of their lives once they reached Ryan Park, she returned to statements she had made to Constance Meaning. She was unready to approach anything resembling truth just yet.

Her attorney listened with interest as she spoke, allowing her to freely express herself. When she paused, as if awaiting his assessment of her discourse, David cleared his throat, looked deeply into her eyes, and, in an unruffled manner stated, "Nora, I have had an opportunity to review the evidence that has been developed against you. You need to understand that the evidence is very damaging. You have listened to Deputy Craig as he spoke from the witness stand, so you are aware of some of the evidence that will be presented to a jury. Within the next few days I will bring to you the full case that the County Attorney will unveil against you. When you have had the opportunity to examine this evidence we will meet again to discuss your opinions and positions. Do you have anything further to discuss during this our first visit?"

Nora thought for a moment, attempting to conceal her fears of the evidence and the thought of reliving the crimes. "Very well," she answered, "I will be here."

"I want you to spend several days reviewing the evidence which, of course, will be in narrative form. Each of the physical exhibits, including witness affidavits, a pistol, a bear's skull, and other items to be admitted as evidence, will be explained in narrative form for you. So, Nora, I will deliver the evidence within a day or so. We have much work to do." David left the interview room, and Nora was escorted back to her cell where she would have ample time to carefully review the meeting with David. Above all, she would need to decide her strategy.

When the evidence was presented to Nora she carefully laid the file folders containing the documents on the cot in her cell. As she viewed the assembled folders that had been so neatly developed, her first thoughts of the evidence were that the folders themselves seemed so neutral, so unthreatening. How could these folders and the contents of the folders contain a force so disturbing that the remainder of her day and days to follow would be so shattered with heavy clouds of fear and uncertainty? With shaking hands, she picked-up a folder, examined the label that described the contents of the file, laid the folder down and picked-up a second folder. Finally, she opened a file labeled "AFFIDAVITS." With trembling hands, she began to read the statement of a witness who described seeing an automobile pulling a trailer into Ryan Park. Other witness statements followed until she read the affidavit that described the black pick-up entering Ryan Park and then leaving with a trailer attached to the pick-up.

Her breathing was nearly labored and her heart pumped rapidly as she read the contents of the remaining file holders. After reading the observations and assumptions presented by Deputy Craig, she was shocked that he had so correctly described her every movement and action. Tears welled her eyes as she read his description of the murder of Deputy Clem Sours. Deputy Craig was correct in every aspect she uttered silently to herself. How would she be able to offer explanations for the soil samples? How would she be able to explain the death of the bear...the pistol with her finger prints...the tissue paper found in Sour's pick-up that contained her DNA? Could she somehow at least defend against the accusations that she had trained the bear to kill Gregorio? Even that small area of doubt, she feared, would be somehow explained. She replaced the documents back into the file holders, carefully placed them in order for further examination, and placed the stack of folders on the floor near her cot.

It was done: she had examined most of the evidence. Some of it she had carefully and thoroughly read; other portions of the evidence, such as the narrative describing the death of Deputy Sours, she hastily scanned. Once the initial impact of her introduction to the evidence had somewhat ebbed, she would again, more thoroughly, examine each document. Her thoughts now turned to her attorney, David Grimley. Was she prepared to discuss the evidence with him? How would she answer his questions as he offered to her each element contained in the evidence? She spent a sleepless night as jumbled thoughts raced through her mind in near panic mode. Was there a strategy? Was there any recourse other than to..................

DEPUTY LENNY CRAIG

Busy with a more normal work routine now that the major elements of the investigation had been completed, Deputy Craig occupied his time with regular patrols of his assigned work area. Now able to stop in and visit with farmers and ranchers, he was able to quickly regain an awareness of activities in his work area.

On his agenda were a number of meetings with the County Attorney as elements of the pending trial were planned. Of particular importance was Deputy Craig's scheduled deposition. While not working or attending to matters of the trial, Deputy Craig was enjoying time with his wife, Kathy.

DELMAR MENTIS

Life at Ryan Park had returned to the routine responsibilities of managing his property and residence. Winter had once again set-in and work activities necessary to live comfortably were of foremost importance. Driving to and from his work place in Laramie occupied much of his time. Delmar, too, was scheduled to participate in depositions.

DAN LASSITER, COUNTY ATTORNEY

The office of the County Attorney was in a status of organized chaos as preparations for the trial gained momentum. Lassiter had chosen aides for specific trial assignments. Each aide was now reviewing evidence and deciding the best approach for scheduling and managing witnesses. Lassiter was also occupied with attempts to locate additional witnesses. Needing to fill in the gaps, represented by insufficient evidence, Lassiter was on the hunt for a witness who may have seen Nora Dolor's green Lincoln, attached to a trailer, parked near the place where Deputy Craig's body had been found. He had placed notices in local news papers asking for anyone who may have seen the Lincoln and trailer on the night of April 30, 1982, to come forth. Next, he had assigned an investigative agent to travel to Pontiac, Michigan to try to locate the owner of the down-and-out circus where the Dubliski's had been staying before traveling to Ryan Park. Should he be able to locate additional witnesses, he would carefully need to navigate the rules of court in order to be able to introduce the "surprise" witnesses.

Lassiter was satisfied with the progress being made for the upcoming trial. The evidence was well organized; physical exhibits were properly labeled and arranged for proper admission; and witness affidavits would soon be supported by depositions. Judge Wolfe, being kept informed of the progress being made by the County Attorney, warned that he did not want to be surprised by any unforeseen stumbling blocks that would impede the outcome of a neat and clean trial.

DAVID GRIMLEY, ATTORNEY

This was a mess, he thought as he paced the floor of his office. Was he concerned that the evidence was so clean and clear cut…so void of any improprieties…that the elements of deceit and fabrication were the basis of the investigation? No, the Sheriff's department would not conduct itself in such a manner. And, he had to admit, the testing of soil samples and ballistic analysis were such that no one could contest the validity of such evidence. Exactly how to defend his client seemed to depend upon her reactions to the evidence and, as well, how she would address each of the accusations being made against her. If she told the truth and admitted to each of the charges, he could explain to her the elements of an Alford plea and then agree to the court's proceedings from that point. Or, he could discuss with her the merits of a plea of guilt by mental illness. Should she--even after admitting her guilt--enter the trial maintaining her plea of not guilty, how would he establish elements of defense that may or may not give her a fair opportunity with a jury? The answers to these questions, he believed, lay entirely with Nora Dolor.

The trial now was scheduled to being in just three weeks. Although he had been meeting with Nora nearly each day, she was no closer to an honest discussion with him than the day of their first meeting. He planned to meet with her this afternoon, and he planned to aggressively confront her. She needed to understand that his decisions as to how to defend her now depended entirely on her answers to each element of evidence.

That afternoon, as David walked to the jail to meet with Nora, his thoughts ranged far and wide. Somewhat alarmed that the trial was quickly approaching and he yet remained undecided as to how to defend her, he convinced himself that today was either a make or break day. He would either make progress toward an appropriate defense or he would consider breaking his agreement to defend this woman.

Nora was in the interview room when David arrived. She sat quietly at the available table: her thoughts were also well aligned with those that David posed to himself.

"Good afternoon, Nora" David felt her eyes examining him as he sat across the table between them. "Hello," she coldly responded.

"Today is the day, Nora, that we have to get down to brass tacks. By that I mean you absolutely must address the evidence with honesty. Thus, I ask you, are the allegations against you true or false? You must answer me, one way or the other."

She sat silent. David did not know if she had answered him with her silence or if she were contemplating an answer.

Then she answered. In her broken English she loudly, almost seeming defiant, stated, "...yes, my God yes, it is all true. The evidence almost seems like the investigators were there, watching me. I am lost. I don't know what to do..."

Stunned...not expecting that answer, David collected his thoughts and began, "...Nora, I confess. I have reviewed the evidence several times and I have tried to visualize some type of defense. Let me now explain the options that I believe to be the only options possible. David then explained the Alford plea and the most likely decision that would be rendered by the court. Then, a plea of not guilty by reason of insanity was explained, again with the most likely decision that would be made by the court. Finally, David advised Nora that she was within her legal rights to maintain a not guilty plea, allowing the trial to continue until such time that the jury was dismissed to deliberate.

Nora sat quietly as she considered each option explained by David. Finally, in a soft, low voice, she stated, "…I will begin the trial with my not guilty plea. I will take my chances."

David nodded in agreement and then responded, "Nora the best that I will be able to do to defend you is to object to both witness statements and the admission of physical exhibits. I can well anticipate the judge's answer: "over ruled." But there may be several areas where I may be able to achieve some doubt in the jury members" minds. Now, on to several other issues. There are some new developments. Although I have not been officially notified, I have heard talk that the County Attorney may have discovered a witness who saw your Lincoln attached to the trailer, parked very near the area where Deputy Sours' body was found. Also, Nora, an investigator is going to Pontiac, Michigan to speak with the owner of a circus where you and your husband lived. These are not good developments. I can object to surprise witnesses, but with little effect. Finally, before I leave, you need to also know that Wyoming law enforcement agents, police and sheriff's deputies in particular, are planning a mass appearance on the first day of your trial. Their purpose, I understand, is to deliver the message that Wyoming law enforcement agencies expect justice to prevail in the death of Deputy Clem Sours. You need to be ready for that when you see the court room packed with law enforcement officers."

Nora stared blankly at the floor. What had she created for herself?

David left the jail feeling somewhat despondent. The cards were stacked against him and the life of his client rested on the unsteady balance of what he might be able to do to create compassion and empathy within the jury…a jury that may well identify with the law enforcement agents who would make a strong appearance at the trial. He now would do what he could do to prepare himself for the trial.

SHERIFF CHESTER OVERMAN

Although the trial was not scheduled for another three weeks, Sheriff Overman conducted several meetings with the deputies of the department. His purpose was to assign each employee with specific roles throughout the trial. He met several times with Judge Wolfe to discuss the security measures necessary to ensure that any and all possibilities of disruption or security breeches would be managed properly. For Sheriff Overman this was not just another trial: this trial, he hoped, would result in a conviction of murder for the person who was accused of Deputy Clem Sours' death.

RAWLINS DAILY NEWS

Citizens of Rawlins have become increasingly aware of the criminal charges that have been filed against a woman identified as Irana Dubliski, also known as Nora Dolor. While the County Attorney, Dan Lassiter, has chosen to divulge only minimal information related to the charges, it is known that the woman is accused of the murder of her husband, a man identified as Gregorio Dubliski. Information that has reached this desk suggests that the defendant had trained a bear to actually kill her husband. The County Attorney has stated that he has sufficient evidence to prove that the woman did, in fact, train the bear. We suspect that will all come out during the trial. To make matters worse for the defendant, she is also accused of the murder of Sheriff Deputy Clem Sours. The last we had heard of the death of Clem Sours, nearly a year ago, was that his death was attributed to suicide. In an interview with the County Coroner, Dr. Purdy, this paper was informed that the cause of Clem Sours' death had been changed to "Possible Murder." We suspect that this will also be resolved during the trial. This paper has been informed that the trial is scheduled to begin in about three weeks. We are also aware that citizens of Rawlins have begun to receive orders to appear for jury duty. With a final word about the defendant we find that her name change to DOLOR is a Spanish word for PAIN. We wonder if there is perhaps a morbid message that will be delivered at the conclusion of the trial.

CHAPTER FIFTEEN
THE TRIAL

Nora Dolor had been held in the County jail for nearly two years while awaiting her day in court. She had proven herself to be trust worthy, polite, and cooperative: all behavioral elements that led to her assignment in the jail kitchen. In addition to her work assignment, she had been granted permission to acquire a few personal items that brought a glimmer of enjoyment to her life. The beauty-aids, in particular, were accepted with relish. She arose early on the day of the trial, and was soon sitting in her cell dressed in an attractive skirt and white blouse; she had carefully combed and prepared her hair in such a manner so as to reveal the results of the make-up she had used. She was an attractive woman, and she hoped that some of the jury members would be impressed with her appearance.

"Okay, Nora," a jail matron summoned. "It's time that we get you over to the courthouse. Here is a little jacket for you to wear—it's cold out today."

She was placed in hand restraints and escorted to the vehicle that would transport her to the courthouse. Once there she was met with a flurry of activity. Two news reporters with cameras who attempted to gain photographs of her when she stepped from the vehicle were shooed away by the escorting deputies. The entrance to the courthouse was lined with law enforcement officers and would-be spectators. Prospective jurors wandered the hall ways waiting for instructions. Sheriff's deputies were busy monitoring a walk-through metal detector as people began to enter the court room. A bailiff, attempting to locate and identify each prospective juror, frantically walked the hall way encouraging his people to follow him to the jury room. Numerous law enforcement officers arriving from various locations in Wyoming were adding to the noisy confusion.

Nora Dolor, wedged between the two escorting deputies, was rapidly whisked through the crowded hallway and taken to a holding area. There she would wait for her attorney and for her entry into the court room.

Noise, congestion, and near pandemonium were soon replaced by a quiet calm as people were seated in the court room or were finally located in the jury room. There were just a few local residents—those who habitually attended trials—who found seats in the court room, otherwise most of the seating was taken by law enforcement officers.

Nora and her attorney, David Grimley, spent just a short time discussing their strategy. Before they were summoned to enter the court room, David explained the routine procedures that the Judge would follow as the trial opened. Upon entering the court room, Nora was immediately overwhelmed with first the number of people present to observe the trial, and second by the physical appearance of the court room.

It was a large room. The Judge's bench sat at the west end of the room. Two tables with chairs were located immediately in front of the Judge's bench: one table for the defendant and one table for the prosecutor. A three-foot high wooden, ornamental fence situated behind the two tables, separated the spectators from the main trial participants. This fence continued from the north side of the room to the south side, and was constructed with a small hinged gate. To the east of the room were located the spectators' seats: a walk-way separated the wooden rows of seats into two units. On the north side of the room were the chairs used by the jury members. The wall behind the chairs for the jury consisted of five large windows. The room, painted in a soft brown color, had been constructed with a space of twelve to fourteen feet from floor to ceiling. Windows and doors were framed with a dark stained wood. Four large fans hung from the ceiling.

David, holding Nora's arm, escorted her into the court room and to the table where they would spend the next two weeks. A sheriff's deputy followed and seated himself near, but not at the table. The court room—except for an occasional cough, whisper, or scuffling of feet—was quiet. About that time the County Attorney and his staff entered the room and took their place at the prosecutor's table. Following the County Attorney were the bailiff and the jury pool. This group of people was seated in the first several rows of seats in the spectator area. Finally, a door behind the

Judge's bench opened and Judge Wolfe entered the court room. A loud "ALL RISE" was given by the bailiff and the trial was underway.

After several words of instructions regarding court room decorum, Judge Wolfe read a prepared statement that explained the charges against Nora Dolor. "Ladies and gentlemen," he addressed to all in the room, "it will soon be the responsibility of the defense attorney and the prosecuting attorney to more thoroughly define the elements on both sides of this trial. These attorneys will do so when they give their opening statements. Before that phase of the trial we will select twelve jury members and two alternate members. Mr. Grimley and Mr. Lassiter, are you ready to begin with jury selection?" Both attorneys affirmed their readiness.

Nora's attorney, in a hushed voice, explained how the selection process would unfold. He advised Nora that he would attempt to "load" his selection choices with women. As each attorney questioned jurors and then challenged the selections made by the opposing attorney, it was not long before a jury was selected. Jurors who were selected took their seats in the jury box. Five males and seven women were seated as members of the jury. The bailiff escorted those in the jury pool who were not selected to the Clerk of Court's office where they were released from jury duty.

"Nora," David whispered, "this phase of the trial is moving along rather quickly. I am satisfied with the selection of the jury. Hopefully, the women on the jury will prove to be of benefit to you. Well, it won't be long before the Judge calls for opening statements."

Shifting nervously in her chair, Nora slightly turned toward the spectators who she found were nearly all watching her. She returned her attention to Judge Wolfe who had begin to read a list of instructions for the jury members. The Judge then read guidelines for the opening statements. Dreading the prosecutors' statements, Nora attempted to divert her thoughts to more pleasant memories. She knew, however, that she had no choice but to listen to each accusation against her.

Judge Wolfe asked Dan Lassiter if he were ready to begin his statements. "Yes, Your Honor," the County Attorney responded. He then turned to the jury members and began, "Ladies and gentlemen, it is now my responsibility to explain to you the evidence that has been collected against the defendant, Nora Dolor, who, incidentally, has changed her name from Irana Dubliski. Nevertheless, the evidence that will be revealed to you will clearly demonstrate that Nora Dolor trained a bear to kill her husband and, then, just a few hours after the murder of her husband, she held a hand gun to the head of Deputy Clem Sours and pulled the trigger."

Dan Lassiter then meticulously described each element of and the manner in which the crimes were committed. As well, he described her use of the trailer and her movement of the trailer, emphasizing her manipulation of Clem Sours in order to silence him from informing his superiors of the information he had collected about Nora and her husband. Before ending his statement, Dan Lassiter informed the jury members that they would hear from a number of witnesses who would offer testimony related to what each witness had personally observed. Finally, Lassiter described each physical exhibit and spoke of how exactly each exhibit linked Nora to the crimes.

During Dan Lassiter's statements, David Grimley followed the statements with a pen that he applied to a note pad. It was now David's statement that the jury would hear. He also began his statements with "Ladies and gentlemen of the jury." Risking the jury's opinion that he actually had no reasonable defense for Nora's crimes, he began, "...now, ladies and gentlemen, I ask you to take a good look at the defendant, Nora Dolor. Does this person—you can see that she is a small woman—look to you like someone who would commit not one but two murders?" He paused for effect, then continued. "Yes, she changed her name, but people all the time change their names. That issue has nothing to do with this case. In fact, her name change was brought up to confuse and cloud real issues. Exactly what are the real issues? Well, let me tell you about real issues. Nora Dolor was an abused woman. Her husband, Gregorio Dubliski, was an alcoholic and a very mean and abusive person. The short time he was in Carbon County he made several enemies, anyone of which could have killed him."

"Yes," he continued, "you will hear from witnesses and you will be presented a number of exhibits. As you hear from witnesses and as you examine exhibits, let me remind you that supposition and conjecture cannot take the place of actual facts. In order for Nora Dolor to be convicted of these crimes, there can be no doubts. Any reasonable doubt is reason for you to return a verdict of not guilty."

David Grimley ended his statements without mentioning the death of Clem Sours. He believed that the evidence regarding Sours' death was too weak, and much conjecture underscored the statements made by the County Attorney about Sours' death. He would wait until witnesses and exhibits were presented before attempting to dislodge the foundations for the murder charge that would be presented by the prosecutor. He understood that his opening statements lacked the necessary strength to sway a jury at the infancy of the trial, but he had few other options.

At the conclusion of the opening statements, Judge Wolfe announced that the trial was in adjournment and would convene the next day at 9 A.M. He addressed Dan Lassiter and instructed him to provide the court with a list of his witnesses and the schedule for each witness. The Judge admonished the jury members to not discuss the trial with anyone and to avoid reading the daily news about the trial. Judge Wolfe rose from the bench. The bailiff loudly shouted, "ALL RISE."

Nora was returned to the jail; she ate a hasty supper; and, then, attempted to relax in the day room. Her attorney stopped in to ask Nora if she had questions or concerns. Nora assured him that she was satisfied with the first day of the trial.

She was up early the next morning. She dressed in the same clothing she had worn the day before, and she applied her make-up so as to again create the best possible appearance. Soon escorting deputies arrived and encouraged her to ready herself for transportation to the courthouse.

Day two of the trial began with the routine protocol. After Judge Wolfe read several instructions that he expected the attorneys to follow, he opened the proceeding for the examination of witnesses.

"Your Honor," Dan Lassiter began, "my first witness will be Delmar Mentis."

"You may call the witness," the Judge directed.

Delmar Mentis entered the witness box and, following the questions given by Dan Lassiter, proceeded to explain his discovery of the body he had found on the hiking trail located above Ryan Park. He spoke of being a member of the Coroner's jury, and how he had identified the hunting arrow point found in the body of the dead man. His final testimony included the discovery of both a broken arrow and the pieces of burlap. When asked to explain the pieces of burlap, Delmar stated that it appeared that the burlap had been used to wrap around shoes or even around the paws of a bear in order to conceal foot prints.

David Grimley challenged the testimony of the broken arrow, wanting to know how the arrow amounted to any semblance of pertinent evidence. Answering, Delmar pointed out that the broken arrow perfectly matched the broken wood that was left in the arrow point. The arrow, Delmar, advised, had been driven into the victim and then broken. When Nora's attorney questioned the testimony of the pieces of burlap, Dan Lassiter interrupted and advised that photographs taken at the murder site would demonstrate the prints left by the burlap. Judge Wolfe over-ruled the objections made by Nora's attorney.

Dan Lassiter than called Dr. Purdy as a witness who described the autopsy performed on the dead man. As well, Dr. Purdy testified about the autopsy performed on Clem Sours. He discussed the arrow point as being the cause of death of Gregorio Dubliski, and stated that a bullet to the head of Clem Sours was the cause of death in that case. When asked why he had changed the reason for Clem Sours' death from suicide to possible murder, Dr. Purdy merely stated that he had been given additional information and that information well indicated that Clem Sours was neither depressed nor despondent at the time of his death. Thus, he believed that Sours had not committed suicide, but had been killed by a gun shot that had been delivered by some person other than Sours.

Nora's attorney's only question for Dr. Purdy was if he knew the identify of the person who had placed the bullet in Sours' head. Dr. Purdy answered that he had no such information.

The next witness called was Deputy Lenny Craig. Attired in his "dress" uniform, Deputy Craig obviously impressed the jury members by his appearance. Dan Lassiter, after laying the foundation to establish Deputy Craig's training and length of service with the Sheriff's department, asked Deputy Craig to explain to the court the elements of his investigation, how the investigation was conducted, and the results of the investigation.

Beginning with the examination of the body found by Delmar Mentis, Craig explained the photographs taken of the body and the area surrounding the body. He emphasized the strange foot prints found as well as the small tennis shoe prints found at the scene. Then, in a very methodical manner, he described each step of the investigation and the discoveries made throughout the course of the investigation. Piece by piece, the jury members were informed of the discovery of the bear carcass; the metal cup attached to a leg of the bear; the theory that the metal cup had been used to deliver the arrow into the victim; the broken arrow and the burlap pieces found near the site where the body was found; and, to underscore his testimony regarding the bear, Deputy Craig went into detail why he believed that the bear had been trained to kill the victim. Before David Grimley was able to enter an objection, Dan Lassiter interrupted Deputy Craig and asked Judge Wolfe for permission to speak with Nora's attorney and the Judge at the bench. Judge Wolfe gave his permission and both attorneys assembled at the Judge's bench where Lassiter informed the Judge that he wished to interrupt Deputy Craig's testimony in order to introduce the witness who would provide testimony that would describe the training of the bear. Although David Grimley objected to this irregularity, Judge Wolfe gave his permission.

Entering the court room was an aged gentleman wearing a much wrinkled, multi-colored cotton shirt, and a pair of patched trousers. He appeared to be in his late seventies, very little hair remained on his shining pate, and his face, adorned with a pair of black glasses, bore the signs of a rough and tumble life. Lassiter invited him to take his place in the witness box; asked him to state his name; and then the Clerk of Court administered the oath. The old man settled into the available chair and waited for Lassiter to begin his questioning.

"Please state your name, Sir, and provide the court with some background information about your-self." Lassiter awaited the old man's answer.

"Well, my name…already gave it to you once…is Henry Cobb. I'm from Pontiac, Michigan where I own a pretty worn-out old circus. I came here to testify about a trailer and a bear that had been stolen from me…"

Lassiter interrupted the old man and asked, "who do you think stole your trailer and the bear?"

"Oh, I know who did that," the old man stated.

"Is that person sitting in the court room today, Sir?" Lassiter asked.

The old man looked around the court room and then centered his gaze on the defense counsel's table. "Yep," he answered. That little woman sitting yonder is one of them who took my trailer and the bear."

"Please, Sir, describe the person you are pointing at…just so that we are sure of the person you believe to be the one who took your trailer and the bear."

Henry Cobb, continuing to point his bony finger at Nora Dolor, offered a description of her clothing and personal appearance.

"Thank you, Sir," Lassiter continued. "Now, please tell the court about how you met Nora Dolor and her husband. Also, tell the court about anything unusual that occurred while they were at your residence."

"Well," the old man began, "…the woman…she called herself Irana Dubliski…and her husband…he called himself Gregorio Dubliski…I think that's what they called themselves…came looking for jobs. I felt sorry for them so I took them in. Gave them a place to stay and offered them what work that I had available. They didn't bother me much and they did the little work that I gave them. I took an interest in the woman because she was caring and kind to the animals that I had. She gave a lot of attention to this one bear that used to be in my circus. She fed it and combed it and just gave it a lot of attention and care. Pretty soon the bear followed her all over the grounds. I didn't have to keep the bear locked away because it became so attracted to her. Well, as time went on I watched the woman with the bear and I started seeing some strange things going on…"

"Objection, Your Honor, the witness has used the term STRANGE without a more specific definition…" Nora's attorney waited for the Judge's response.

"Over ruled," the Judge finally answered. "Let the witness finish his statement…we will see if he clarifies the word he used."

Lassiter apologized to the witness and urged him to continue.

"Okay," the old man cleared his throat and began…"as I was saying, I started seeing some strange things that she was doing with the bear. She sat up an old circus dummy that I once used…it was a figure of a man dressed in a colorful costume…anyway, I watched her as she brought the bear near the dummy and when the bear was within reach of the dummy, she would take the bear's front leg and shove it against the dummy. Every day she repeated this with the bear and each time that the bear shoved its front leg against the dummy she would give the bear some sort of a treat. Pretty darn soon the bear was doing this on its own. After a week or so I noticed that she had attached some sort of a can…at least it looked like a metal can to me…to the front leg of the bear. I also noticed that she had placed what looked like an arrow into the can. Then when the bear shoved its front leg toward the dummy the arrow stuck into the dummy. As time went on…maybe three weeks or so…I watched her pour some sort of liquid on the ground, just next to the dummy. She would then leave the area and open a gate so that the bear could enter. Sometimes she would walk along with the bear and hold the bear's head down to where he could smell whatever she had poured on the ground. Then, she would again direct the bear to shove the arrow-looking thing into the dummy. It was not long, maybe a week, that the bear would go directly to the dummy, smell the ground, and shove the shaft into the dummy. It was the darnedest thing that I ever saw. I've been around a lot of circus animals and helped with a lot of training, but she did some things that I never knew was possible."

"Very well, Mr. Cobb. Your testimony has been very helpful. Now, will you tell the court about when the trailer and bear disappeared?"

The witness thought for a moment and said, "…It was about four months, I suspect, that I could tell that the man, Gregorio, was getting antsy. I figured that they were about ready to pull out. I got up one morning and when I went out onto my property I noticed that a nice little, white trailer was gone. I got to looking around and soon discovered that the bear that Irana had been working with was also gone. Both the man and woman were also gone, so it didn't take much to figure out that they had stolen my trailer and the bear." The old man sat and waited for further questions or instructions.

"I have no further questions of this witness, Your Honor," Lassiter addressed the judge. "Mr. Grimley," the Judge called to Nora's attorney, "do you have questions of the witness?"

Grimley stood and walked to the witness box. "Mr. Cobb, I am Nora Dolor's attorney. I have just a few questions. First, Mr. Cobb, how were you able to observe Nora as she worked with the bear?"

Cobb answered curtly, "…well, I had a bunch of windows in the little apartment where I lived and I could see what was taking place all about my property. It didn't take much effort to watch her leave the room where she and her husband were staying and walk to the cages where the animals were kept. I could easily watch her every day that she worked with that bear."

"Thank you, Mr. Cobb," Grimley responded. "Now, and I certainly do not want to infer that I do not believe your testimony, but how are the jury members to believe who you say you are and believe what you have testified to today?"

"I ain't much, but I'm who I say I am," Mr. Cobb retorted. His comments raised a ripple of stifled laughs from the spectators. "I ain't got much, but I do have most of that old circus. It still puts a few dollars in my pocket. When the County Attorney contacted me and told me that my trailer was in the custody of the Sheriff I agreed to come out here and try to get my trailer. I also agreed to be here in court today and tell what I knew of the people who stole my trailer and the bear. That's about all that I can say."

"Thank you, Mr. Cobb, I have no further questions." Grimley returned to his chair and gave Nora an unconvincing smile. Nora sat rigidly in her chair. She was stunned by Henry Cobb's testimony, testimony that she had not anticipated.

"Your Honor," Dan Lassiter politely addressed the Judge, "I can see that the day is wearing on. Shall I place Deputy Craig back on the witness stand? Or would you rather adjourn the court for today?"

"Yes, the day is about worn-out," the Judge responded. "Let's do just that. We will adjourn now and convene tomorrow morning at 9 A.M. sharp." The Judge then gave the routine admonishments to the jury members and rose from his seat. "ALL RISE!" shouted the bailiff.

Nora Dolor spent the evening and night recalling the simple testimony of Henry Cobb. She had nearly forgotten this old man, and then to see him enter the court room sent a sense of doom into her soul. Would this be the testimony that would possibly end her life?

Court began on the third day as court had begun the two days before. After spectators, now fewer in number as many of the law enforcement agents had departed, jury members, attorneys, and the Judge had taken their respective places in the court room, the trial convened. Dan Lassiter called Deputy Lenny Craig to return to the witness box and testimony began. Nora Dolor sat nervously and tensely as she awaited more testimony from Lenny Craig. She appeared tired and adrift as she stared out of the windows wishing she were in a better place.

"Now, Deputy Craig," Dan Lassiter began, "we will return to your testimony regarding the investigation and the results of that investigation. I warn you that as you testify I will interrupt you at proper times to obtain permission to enter physical exhibits."

No sooner had Deputy Craig begun to offer testimony regarding photographs than Dan Lassiter obtained permission to enter a number of photographs—including photographs of the victim lying on the walking trail; photographs of the foot prints; photographs of a broken arrow and pieces of burlap; and photographs of the bear carcass—were given to the jury members.

David Grimley offered a number of objections as he challenged the veracity of the exhibits. His objections were over-ruled when Dan Lassiter provided documents from the crime lad proving that the photographs had been officially taken and processed, with proper chain of evidence.

At this time, for whatever reason, Nora's attorney challenged Craig's assumption that the bear had been trained to kill the victim. This challenge was over-ruled when the Judge reminded Grimley that a witness had credibly testified that he had witnessed the training of the bear. The Judge advised Grimley to keep abreast of the court proceedings so that his objections would be pertinent and timely.

Once the photographs had been distributed to the jury, Craig continued his testimony. He resumed his statements with descriptions of the movement of the trailer on the night of April 30. At this time Lassiter introduced the affidavits submitted by witnesses who had seen the trailer move in and out of Ryan Park. These witnesses would be called later.

Craig then went into a detailed explanation of the facts that had led him to understand the movements and actions of Irana Dubliski that night, including her scheme to lure Deputy Clem Sours into her grasps. He followed these explanations with descriptions of the search for the bear's skull, the search of the trailer, finding the gun in the trailer, and finding clumps of hair from the bear that had been hauled in the trailer. To further prove that the trailer and Clem Sours' pick-up had been on the Forest road just below where the body of Gregorio Dubliski was found, Craig told the jury about the dried mud and dirt samples taken from the trailer and from the pick-up and how those samples matched the mud and dirt samples taken from the forestry road.

Awaiting objections from Nora's attorney, Dan Lassiter turned to Deputy Craig and asked Craig to give further information about the bear's skull, the pistol found in the trailer, the importance of the trailer in the case, and evidence found in Deputy Sours' pick-up.

The trailer, Craig explained, was used to haul the trained bear. Craig further explained that once the defendant and her husband arrived in Ryan Park, Nora Dolor believed that the area was perfect for carrying out her long-planned act to kill her husband. Thus, the trailer hauled the bear throughout Ryan Park and eventually on to the forestry road where Nora Dolor opened the trailer door and released the bear so that it could complete the act as it had been trained by Nora Dolor.

Deputy Craig, explaining that Nora Dolor, after using the bear to kill her husband, had to dispose of the bear. She did so by using a .38 caliber pistol that was found in the trailer. The pistol contained her finger prints. In order to prove that the bear had been purposely killed, the bear's skull had to be found. And, when it was found, it contained the .38 caliber bullet. Crime lab ballistics, Craig stated, proved the link between the pistol found in the trailer and the slug found in the skull.

Finally, Deputy Craig began his testimony with information he had pieced together about the death of Clem Sours. As Dan Lassiter distributed photographs of the scene where Sours' body had been found, Craig told the jury that he was convinced that Sours was not suicidal, rather he was enamored with Nora Dolor. He had no reason to kill himself, Craig told the jury. As the photographs of Sours sitting in the pick-up, slumped over the steering wheel were given to the jury, several of the females in the jury winced and quickly passed the photographs on to the next juror. During the time that Craig's testimony lagged for several moments, Nora Dolor sat uneasily in her chair, visibly upset by the testimony that Craig had given.

Continuing, Craig told the jury that Sours was most likely falling in love with Nora Dolor, why would he kill himself? He then went into detail as he spoke of the time frame for the death of Nora Dolor's husband and the death of Deputy Sours. It was not just coincidence that Sours died just shortly after the death of Gregorio Dubliski, Craig told the jury, but a sequence of events committed by the same person. As far as evidence found in Sours' pick-up, Craig had to admit that there were no finger prints; but, he emphasized, a tissue paper that contained Nora Dolor's DNA was found in the cab of the pick-up. That, he told the jury, was specific evidence to prove that Nora Dolor had been in Sours' pick-up.

Again, Dan Lassiter paused the testimony of Deputy Craig in order to introduce Stanley Brown as a witness who had seen and stopped on the highway to investigate a green Lincoln attached to a white trailer. Over-ruling David Grimley's objection to the examination of this witness, Judge Wolfe allowed Lassiter to examine the witness.

Following the oath given by the Clerk of Court, Lassiter approached the witness box and began his questioning. "Mr. Brown, please introduce yourself…tell the court a little about yourself."

"My name is Stanley Brown. I live over in Encampment where I run a little cow and calf operation. I also work part-time in the hard ware store in Saratoga."

"Thank you, Sir, now, will you please tell the court where you were late on April 30 of last year?" Lassiter, turning to the defense table, waited for the witness to answer.

"Hmmm," Mr. Brown thought. "…On April 30 I had been over near Cheyenne where I bought two calves. I had loaded them in a horse trailer that I was pulling with my pick-up. I stopped in Laramie for a quick sandwich, and then headed over the Snowy Range road on my way home. I was about two miles or so from the turn-off to Ryan Park when I came up on a car pulling a white trailer. The vehicles were parked on the side of the road, headed in the direction that I just came from." Mr. Brown paused and raised a glass of water to his mouth.

Lassiter gave him time to finish his drink and then asked, "About what time was that when you encountered the car and the trailer? Also, Sir, what did you do, if anything when you saw the car and the trailer?"

"It was getting late and I wanted to get home to unload the calves. I remember looking at my watch not long before I saw the car and the trailer. I remember that it was about 11:30. I noticed that the car and the trailer both had emergency flashers on, so I decided that I better stop and check to see if the driver needed help. By the time that I got my pick-up stopped I was forty or fifty feet beyond where the car and trailer were parked. I walked back to the car and trailer and knocked on the driver's side window.

No one answered. I looked into the car but no one was there. I thought that it was very strange that there was no one in the car. I walked around the car and the trailer, but I didn't see anything unusual, such as a flat tire."

Lassiter interrupted Mr. Brown to ask if he remembered about where the car and the trailer were parked.

"I recall," Mr. Brown answered, "that the vehicles were parked on a wide spot on the side of the road. The vehicles were well off the highway. I did notice that just behind the trailer, maybe fifteen or twenty feet, a rough looking road led up into the timber. It looked to me like an old logging road. That's about it, I guess. I did think that maybe the driver had begun to walk back to Ryan Park. So, I returned to my pick-up and drove on down to Ryan Park. I didn't see anyone walking on the road."

"Thank you, Mr. Brown. I have no further questions." Lassiter turned to the defendant's table waiting for Attorney Grimley to cross-examine the witness.

Mr. Brown, I have just a few questions," Grimley said as he walked away from his table. "First, what transpired to bring you here as a witness today?"

"I read an ad in the paper that asked for anyone who was on the road between Laramie and Ryan Park on April 30 to contact the County Attorney. So, I contacted the County Attorney and told him about my trip from the Cheyenne area," Mr. Brown answered.

"Do you personally know the County Attorney? And if so are you his friend?" Grimley asked.

"No, Sir," Brown answered, "I know of him, but I have never met him before I answered his ad."

"Are you a law enforcement officer, Mr. Brown?" Grimley asked, obviously searching for additional questions.

"No, I am not a law enforcement officer," Mr. Brown answered now understanding the Attorney's direction.

"Mr. Brown," Grimley continued, "do you know Nora Dolor? Have you ever met her before? And, did you see her the night of April 30 when you stopped to check the vehicle and the trailer?"

"No" Mr. Brown answered, "…I do not know her. I have never met her. I did not see her the night I stopped to check the car and the trailer."

"Thank you, Mr. Brown. Just one more question. Will you describe the car and the trailer that you saw that night?" Grimley awaited Mr. Brown's answer.

"The car was a green Lincoln. I was able to see the color due to the light provided by the flashers. The trailer was a two axle, white in color." Mr. Brown answered.

"Thank you, Mr. Brown. I have no further questions." Grimley returned to the defendant's table.

Dan Lassiter approached the witness and asked him if he was positive that the car was a green Lincoln. Mr. Brown assured him that he was positive that the car was a Lincoln. Lassiter then turned to the jury and said: "Ladies and gentlemen, what you have just heard is very, very important. Evidence indicates that Clem Sours met his death on or about April 30, at about 11:45 P.M. or midnight. Clem Sours sat in his pick-up--a pick-up that he had driven up that rough road that Mr. Brown has just described—and just above the high way where the green Lincoln was parked, Clem Sours met his death. The investigation has also resulted in information about the green Lincoln: a vehicle that Gregorio and Irana Dubliski had rented in Pontiac, Michigan. We have proof that Irana Dubliski drove that vehicle, and we are certain that it was Irana Dubliski who was driving that Lincoln and pulling that trailer on the night of April 30. After Clem Sours was killed, Irana Dubliski drove the Lincoln with the trailer attached to a camp ground just a few miles from where Mr. Brown spotted the vehicles sitting on the road, and at that camp ground she unhooked the trailer, left it in the camp ground, and she left Carbon County on her way to Omaha, Nebraska.

"Objection, Your Honor…Mr. Lassiter has given a statement to the jury based solely on conjecture," Grimley nearly shouted.

"Sustained," the Judge answered. "I can hear you very well, Mr. Grimley. You do not have to shout at me. Now, Mr. Lassiter let's keep your conclusions well founded in fact."

At that point a jury member waved a piece of paper to gain the judge's attention. The judge instructed the bailiff to obtain the paper and deliver it to the judge. After reading the paper, the judge announced: ladies and gentlemen, the jury members have asked that they be given the opportunity to visit the area that the witness described where he saw the vehicle and trailer parked. I am going to recess this hearing for an hour while I speak with the attorneys.

"ALL RISE," the bailiff shouted as the judge left the bench. "Come into my office," the judge called to the attorneys as he left the court room.

In the judge's office, the judge asked Lassiter and Grimley if they had any objection to taking the jury members to the area that had just been described by the witness. Both attorneys agreed that the jury members should have the opportunity to visit the area. Grimley stated that his client, Nora Dolor, should also be included in the viewing of the area. Lassiter stated that he would agree but that Nora Dolor would have to be transported in a vehicle separate from the jury members, and that she would have to be kept at a distance from the jury members as they inspected the area. After some discussion the judge and attorneys came to an agreement as to how transportation and viewing of the area would take place.

Upon returning to the court room, the judge advised the jury members that he would now recess the hearing in order to make arrangements for transporting the jury members and Nora Dolor to the high way where the witness viewed and inspected the vehicle and trailer. "Tomorrow morning, ladies and gentlemen of the jury, please arrive at the courthouse at 7:00 o"clock sharp. Better wear some warm coats; bring a jug of hot coffee; and bring a snack if you choose. I will have a small bus available for transportation. For your information, the defendant will also accompany us, but she will be transported in a separate vehicle and she will remain separate from the jury. Please do not attempt to speak with her or to interact with her in any manner."

Court was adjourned and all participants departed the courthouse. Nora Dolor was escorted back to the jail where her attorney instructed her as to her responsibilities during the venture.

A TRIP TO THE AREA WHERE THE VEHICLE AND TRAILER WERE OBSERVED

The following morning the jury members had collected themselves near the front door of the courthouse. Lassiter and Grimley had arrived just before the jury began to assemble. Judge Wolfe soon exited the courthouse door and advised that the bus would arrive shortly. Then, the bus--and following the bus was a sheriff's vehicle in which two deputies and Nora

Dolor were riding-- parked on the street in front of the courthouse waited the entry of the jury. The jury members entered the bus and Lassiter and Grimley entered Lassiter's personal vehicle. The group were then on their way to Ryan Park. After a ride of about an hour the caravan arrived at the place on the high way where the witness stated that he had stopped to investigate the parked vehicles.

A grey and cloudy day greeted the group as they stepped from the vehicles. Wind rattled the pine trees on each side of the highway. Jury members donned gloves and buttoned coats. Two deputies and Nora Dolor stood well apart from the jury. She had been placed in hand restraints just before leaving the jail. Judge Wolfe addressed the jury: "Well, we made it without a hitch," he began. "Just a few words to guide our progress. First, Dan Lassiter will instruct us on the various components of this outing. Second, unfortunately, I cannot allow any of you to ask questions of Lassiter, Grimley, or me. You will have to make your own observations and draw your own conclusions. Finally, I ask you to not discuss any issues or ask any questions of your jury peers. I will allow you to make written notes. Now, let us listen to Dan Lassiter."

Lassiter, now standing before the jury members, began by stepping-out where the green Lincoln and trailer had been parked. They were all assembled on the wide portion of the high way. "This area here is where the witness saw the vehicle and trailer parked. Walking a few feet behind where the trailer had been parked, he pointed to the rough logging road on which Clem Sours had driven his pick-up. "Now," he stated, "look up to the west, up through those pine trees. Up there is where Clem Sours' pick-up was found. You can well see that the distance from where the Lincoln and trailer were parked and where Sours' pick-up was found is not far at all. It would have been an easy task to walk from the pick-up back to the Lincoln and trailer. Let us now walk the short distance up this road to where the pick-up was found. Watch your step as the road is rough and old tree roots will get you tangled-up."

Lassiter led the group up the road, carefully picking his way through ruts and exposed tree roots. Once at the place where Sours' pick-up had been discovered, he stopped and began a short explanation of how the pick-up had been found. He mentioned that the key to the ignition switch was turned on and the radio had been playing at the time of Sours' death.

By the time that the pick-up was found the battery was "dead." "If Sours had killed himself," he asked the jury, "why would he have left the pick-up running with the radio playing?"

"Let's be cautious of the suppositions and innuendo being interjected into the discovery of the pick-up," Grimley interrupted. "We don't know why Sours had driven his pick-up here and we don't know what he did while he was here."

"As I said at the beginning, the jury members must make their own observations and draw their own conclusions," Judge Wolfe warned.

"Very well," Lassiter stated, "Now, if everyone is ready let us retrace our steps back to the highway. As you walk the distance back to the highway count the number of steps you take just so that you have an idea of the distance that whoever was with Sours that night had to walk. I have walked it several times…I even walked the distance once in full darkness…it is not far and I had no trouble walking the distance in the darkness."

All the while Lassiter was informing the jury members of the particulars of the site where Sours' pick-up was found, Nora Dolor stood at some distance, with a deputy sheriff on either side of her. She was unable to clearly hear Lassiter, but her thoughts were centered on the night that she rode up the rough road to this very spot. Her body trembled with a cold chill, not from the wind that buffeted her, but from her recollection of that night when she was with Sours.

The group made their way down the road and back to the van. At the van, the judge stopped, hesitated, and made one suggestion. "Without violating court guidelines I will ask if any of you wish to see anything further."

One jury member asked, "before we head back to Rawlins can we see the place where the trailer was left?"

"Yes, I understand that the parking area is just a mile or so to the south of us. We can drive down there and then turn around and head back to Rawlins," the judge answered.

As the jury members prepared to enter the van, Lassiter made a final comment: "Ladies and gentlemen, you have seen the place where the Lincoln and the trailer were parked. You saw the place where Sours' pick-up was found. Now, it is up to you to come to terms as to why the Lincoln and the trailer were parked at this spot at the same time that Sours' pick-up was parked up that old road. The witness stated that the caution lights were blinking when he stopped to investigate the vehicle and trailer. Someone knew that they would not be away from the vehicle and trailer for any length of time."

"As a rebuttal to that remark, let me just add that we don't know for certain when the vehicle and trailer were parked here and we don't know the time and for how long Sours' pick-up had been in that spot that we just visited," Grimley responded.

"Aha…." Lassiter hissed, "the witness told us the time he stopped at the vehicle and trailer, and the Coroner told us the time of Sours' death. The vehicle and trailer were parked here during the time limits that have been given to us. The vehicle and trailer and Sours' pick-up were here at the same time."

"Okay," the judge interjected, "those issues must be decided by the jury at the proper time. Now, let's drive on down the road to that place where the trailer was found.

The van, followed by the sheriff's vehicle, entered the drive into the camp ground where the trailer had been found and then turned onto the road that would take them back to the courthouse. At the courthouse the judge advised that trial would reconvene the next day at 8 a.m.

BACK IN THE COURT ROOM

After reconvening the court proceedings, Judge Wolfe instructed Dan Lassiter to proceed with his examination of the witness.

Lassiter put Deputy Craig back on the witness stand and It was now David Grimley's turn to question Deputy Craig. His questioning basically consisted of a series of accusations that the basis for Craig's evidence was pure conjecture and supposition. Craig responded with references to crime lab testing, ballistics tests, finger print comparisons, the testimony of Henry Cobb, the affidavits of witnesses who had seen the green Lincoln pulling the white trailer into Ryan Park and leaving without the trailer, and the witnesses who had seen the black pick-up enter without a trailer but left pulling a white trailer. Nora's attorney then suggested that Deputy Craig was biased as a law enforcement officer and testified to impress the law enforcement spectators. Craig calmly pointed out that his investigation was conducted scientifically and according to all rules that govern investigations. He further stated that his investigatory results were tested and documented by the crime lab.

Finally, Deputy Craig was released as a witness, but with the possibility of being recalled. The next witnesses were those men who had witnessed the movement of the trailer. The first to testify was John Morgan, a Saratoga resident. He took the witness stand, gave his name, and was administered the oath.

Dan Lassiter began his questioning, first by walking back and forth before the witness, tapping a pencil against is temple. "Tell me, Mr. Morgan, where were you on the night of April 30, a year ago?"

"I was sitting at the café in Ryan Park having a late supper. My friends and I had been fishing and hiking all day and on the way home we stopped at the café for a sandwich," Mr. Morgan responded.

"What type of night was it, if you recall?" Lassiter posed.

"Well, I remember that it was dark and there was a very light rain, almost just a mist," Mr. Morgan answered.

"And, what did you see that night?" Lassiter questioned.

"My two friends, Ed Downs and Jim Dustin, and I were sitting by the windows on the north side of the room. We were just chatting and having a cold drink. Occasionally, we would look out of the window to check the rain. It was probably about 10:30 or so when we saw a vehicle. It looked like a green colored vehicle and it was pulling a white trailer. It was maybe half hour or forty-five minutes that we saw the same car come back, but without the trailer. Then, oh…maybe forty minutes or so, we saw a black pick-up pull into Ryan Park and continue up the road. It wasn't half an hour later that we saw the same black pick-up leave Ryan Park; but, this time the pick-up was pulling a white trailer." John Morgan had completed his testimony and waited for Nora Dolor's attorney to cross-examine him.

"Mr. Morgan," David Grimley began, "who was in those vehicles that you described?"

"We couldn't determine who was in the vehicles, but we thought one person was in the car pulling the trailer. We couldn't see who was in the pick-up." Mr. Morgan waited for additional questions.

"So, you were unable to determine who was in either vehicle? Is that correct?" Grimley challenged.

"Yes, that is what I said," Mr. Morgan responded.

"If you were unable to see who was in the vehicles, how could you describe the vehicles? Grimley again challenged.

"Across the road from the café is a neon street light. The car and the pick-up drove beneath that light. Were able to clearly see the vehicles. We couldn't see the interior of the vehicles." Mr. Morgan answered.

"Finally, Mr. Morgan, please look to the defendant's table there…" Grimley pointed to the table… "Was the woman sitting there seen in either of those two vehicles? Think carefully, about your answer."

John Morgan looked carefully at the defendant's table. He then answered, "As I said, we could not see the interior of the vehicles. I don't know if that lady was in one of the vehicles."

"But you did not see her in either vehicle, is that correct?" Grimley further challenged

"No, I did not see her in either vehicle," Mr. Morgan testily answered.

"Thank you, Mr. Morgan. I have no further questions." Grimley turned and returned to his chair at the defendant's table. Nora Dolor had nervously followed the testimony of the witness and closed her eyes as she remembered that night. She had been certain that no one had seen the movement of her vehicle and the trailer.

Dan Lassiter decided to not further question John Morgan. He believed that he had sufficiently proven that it was Nora Dolor's vehicle that entered Ryan Park pulling a white trailer. He would further emphasize that point with the next two witnesses. The jury, he believed, would have no difficulty deciding that if the vehicle belonged to Nora Dolor then the driver obviously had to be Nora Dolor.

The next two witnesses offered testimony similar to the testimony given by John Morgan. Cross examination by David Grimley again centered on their statements that they had not seen Nora Dolor in the vehicles. Dan Lassiter was satisfied that he had placed Nora Dolor at the scene of the murder of her husband.

As each witness finished their testimony, Dan Lassiter reminded the jury members that: "We know who rented the green Lincoln. It was Gregorio Dubliski and Irana Deubliski. No one else drove the Lincoln. Only Irana and Gregorio Dubliski drove that Lincoln. On the evening of April 30, a year ago, both Gregorio and Irana Dubliski were in the Lincoln when it entered Ryan Park towing the trailer. Only Irana Dubliski was in the Lincoln when it was seen leaving Ryan Park. Where was Gregorio Dubliski? He was lying dead on that hiking trail with an arrow point in his heart."

David Grimley objected, basing his objection on conjecture. This time Judge Wolfe over-ruled the objection, stating sufficient ground-work had been laid to establish in whose hands the Lincoln rested.

Lassiter than informed Judge Wolfe that there were no further witnesses. The trial, now in process for twelve days, was nearing the time for closing arguments and the Judge's instructions for the jury. Following the testimony of the last three witnesses, Judge Wolfe adjourned the court for three days, allowing attorneys to prepare for closing remarks.

Nora, exhibiting obvious depression, was escorted back to the country jail. She was disappointed that her attorney had not better represented her, yet she considered the acts that she had committed and well understood that any fault that she attributed to her attorney lay with her. In a mental haze she attended her work duties in the jail kitchen. She cleaned her jail cell and arranged and organized her belongings, all completed in a robotic manner. Her thoughts remained on the trail and the evidence presented to the jury. She thought about the members of the jury and was unable to glean even a suggestion of what each member may be thinking. She slept poorly, often waking only to weep until she would fall into an unsettled sleep. Time passed slowly those three days of court recess. Time that was filled with anguish and despondency.

Tuesday morning arrived, cold and windy. Dark clouds greeted each member of the court proceedings. As Dan Lassiter and David Grimley arrived at the courthouse door they gave one another a brief nod and a "...good morning..." By 9 A.M. Nora was sitting at her place at the defendant's table. Her attorney was occupied with finishing his notes for his closing remarks. Dan Lassiter was working in a similar manner.

Then, "ALL RISE," the bailiff shouted as Judge Wolfe entered the court room through the door behind the Judge's bench. Spectators, including law enforcement agents, quietly sat awaiting the resumption of the trial.

"Good morning," Judge Wolfe addressed the assembled group. "This morning we will hear the closing statements of Dan Lassiter and David Grimley. I anticipate those statements to conclude about noon. We will recess at that point to return about 1:30 this afternoon, at that time I will have the Clerk of Court distribute the jury instructions. I will discuss those in more detail at the appropriate time. Now, Mr. Lassiter and Mr. Grimley, are you both prepared to present your closing remarks?"

When both attorneys answered affirmatively, Judge Wolfe invited Dan Lassiter to begin. Rising from his chair at his table, Dan Lassiter approached the sitting jurors. He purposefully and slowly walked to the far end of the jury box, turned and retraced his steps...all the while looking directly at each juror. "Ladies and gentlemen," he began, "this has been a most difficult time for each of you. Sitting here for nearly two weeks-- listening to the witness testimony and examining exhibits—has not been an easy task. We have now reached the end of this trial, and I ask you to lend me your attention one last time. I want to begin with a brief discussion of the green Lincoln. Deputy Clem Sours watched that Lincoln enter Saratoga. We learned, by reading Deputy Sours' official duty diary, that it was Irana Dubliski, now known as Nora Dolor, who drove the Lincoln into Saratoga. We learned, by watching a surveillance tape at a local gas station in Saratoga, that Deputy Sours filled her tank with gasoline. Irana Dubliski was the one who drove the Lincoln because her husband, an alcoholic, was unable to safely drive the car."

Lassiter paused, looked to the defendant's table to see Nora Dolor with her head down, not watching the proceedings. He continued, "...we also learned by reading Deputy Sours' official notes, that Gregorio and Irana Dubliski had rented that Lincoln in Pontiac, Michigan. No one else drove that Lincoln. We know that it was Nora Dolor who drove the Lincoln, towing the trailer, into Ryan Park. We know that she parked the Lincoln and the trailer at the trail head below where the victim's body was found. For whatever reason, Gregorio Dubliski began walking up that trail. As he did so, she opened the door to the trailer and released the bear, an animal trained by Nora Dolor to deliver an arrow into a specific target...the target, of course, was Gregorio Dubliski. The bear returned to the trailer and was placed back into the trailer. Nora Dolor, then, walked up the trail, and when she found the body, she walked around her dead husband—leaving her shoe prints."

Collecting his thoughts, Lassiter continued, "...Nora Dolor then drove the Lincoln and trailer into a ditch; unhooked the trailer; and drove back to the cabin where she and her late husband were staying. At the cabin she telephoned Clem Sours and told him she needed his help. Nora Dolor then walked the distance back to the trailer and waited for Deputy Sours. Ladies and gentlemen…you heard the witnesses! Those witnesses told you that they saw a black pick-up enter Ryan Park. Clem Sours owned and drove a black pick-up. I might add that crime lab soils tests confirm that Sours' pick-up had been on that forest road. Let's return to Sours' entry into Ryan Park and his arrival at the forest road. Once he located Nora Dolor, he connected the trailer to his pick-up and began to drive back to Ryan Park. Nora Dolor, when they reached a place to turn the pick-up around, stopped their progress; got out of the pick-up; went to the rear of the trailer and released the bear. At that place Nora Dolor killed the bear, purely to conceal evidence. Later, the Forestry Department found the carcass of that bear. Hair samples taken from the carcass exactly match hair samples taken from the trailer."

"Who else" Lassiter continued, "would be driving the Lincoln? Absolutely no one. Nora Dolor drove that Lincoln into Ryan Park and out of Ryan Park. You heard Henry Cobb, the owner of the circus, who told you how Nora Dolor had trained the bear. Nora Dolor planned and eventually completed her objective of killing her husband. Planning, intent, and actually committing the crime equals first degree murder."

"So now we arrive at the death of Deputy Clem Sours," Lassiter then began to reveal his conclusions about Sours' death. "Again, the green Lincoln becomes a very important issue. You heard John Morgan testify about seeing the Lincoln parked on the side of the road, just a few miles south of Ryan Park. That Lincoln, towing the white trailer, was parked just below the site where Deputy Sours' body was found. Coincidence? Hardly! We learned by reading Sours' official duty diary that he had discovered that the Dubliskis were illegally in the United States. Gregorio Dubliski was wanted in Russia for the murder of a policeman. Nora Dolor feared that Deputy Sours would soon report her and her husband to his superiors. She lured Deputy Sours—probably with a lot of sweet talk—into her plot to silence him. She parked the Lincoln along the road, entered Sours' waiting pick-up, and rode with him up that rough road described by Mr. Morgan. Once the pick-up was parked, she took Deputy Sours' service pistol and placed a bullet in his head. This she did within less than two hours after her husband was killed by the trained bear. After killing Sours, she walked back to the Lincoln. Then, after parking the trailer in a nearby camp ground, she was on her way to Omaha, Nebraska."

"That's it, members of the jury," Lassiter faced the jury and began his final summation. "Please do not be misled by the defense attorney's attempt to discredit the evidence by telling you that Nora Dolor had nothing to do with either death. He will attempt to sway your thinking with his assumption that she is innocent because no one had seen her either in Ryan Park or at the place where Clem Sours was killed. I guarantee you that Nora Dolor was responsible for both her husband's death and the death of Clem Sours. In fact, she is guilty of the premediated and malicious death of both men. Thank you."

As he started to walk back to his table, Lassister turned once again to the jury members. "One more thing that I wish to share with you." He paused…. "Over the time that I have reviewed and analyzed the evidence, I have put together a little analogy that I thought would reveal additional clarity about the feelings and thoughts of Nora Dolor. In Italy, during World War Two, there was this person who had wiggled his way into governmental leadership. His name was Benito Mussolini. He was a harsh leader who was piece by piece dismantling the laws of Italy. He was also involved in changing the way the Italian people were to be managed. One of the statements that he made about his destruction of Italy's laws and government was that: 'When you pluck a chicken remove one feather at a time and no one will notice.' Well, I began thinking about Nora Dolor's activities leading up to the death of her husband and the death of Clem Sours. She thought that through the course of her planning, training of the bear, and her intentional manipulation of Clem Sours no one would ever recognize her as the perpetrator of her acts, and that no one would notice. The evidence that has been collected most certainly speaks to her actual involvement. She left several piles of chicken feathers and we now know what the chicken looks like. Thank you, Ladies and Gentlemen. That is all I have."

Lassiter returned to his table amid the rustling of papers from the defendant's table. David Grimley now took his place before the jurors. "Ladies and gentlemen," he began, "this has been a long two weeks. We still have some work to do. Let me begin by saying that it is extremely important that Nora Dolor was never seen at or near the scenes of the murders. The fact that she was never seen raises doubts about her actual participation. And, doubt, jury members, is a condition that you must weigh in your deliberations. Regarding the exhibits, that evidence itself does not include eye witness accounts of Nora Dolor's participation. The evidence presented against her is basically based on supposition and conjecture. Nora Dolor is innocent of these crimes and your verdict must so demonstrate. Before I conclude, I take exception to the analogy that Mr. Lassister has used to compare the tyrant Benito Mussolini with my client, Nora Dolor. For the record, I approach the Honorable Judge Wolfe with my strenuous objection to Mr. Lassister's analogy and ask that the record be stricken of his comments." Grimley then thanked the jury members and turned to await Judge Wolfe's decision regarding his just made objections.

It was just a moment or two before Judge Wolfe gently tapped his gavel, cleared his throat, and addressed David Grimley. "Mr. Grimley, I have often heard attorneys who have carefully phrased an analogy to establish a certain point. In Mr. Lassiter's case, I did not hear him say that Nora Dolor was Benito Mussolini or vice versa. He merely pointed out that their handling of certain activities may have been similar. Your objection is dismissed."

Nora's attorney's comments had been brief, because he did not want to chance making a statement that would possibly reveal an opening for Dan Lassiter.

"Mr. Lassiter," Judge Wolfe called, "do you intend to make any rebuttal statements?"

"No, Your Honor," Lassiter answered. "I have finished."

Judge Wolfe then addressed the attorneys and the jury, advising that jury instructions would be distributed by the Clerk of Court. Once the instructions were in the hands of each juror, the Judge instructed the bailiff to escort the jury to the jury room for their deliberations. "Take your time, you have much information to review. If you have questions, write them on a piece of paper and give the paper to the bailiff."

The jury soon began the deliberation process. At the end of the day with no verdict, the Judge recessed court until the next morning.

Later, back in her jail cell, Nora was told by a jail matron that the jury had not yet reached a verdict. She waited patiently throughout that day and part of the following day. About 1 P.M. that afternoon, Nora was told that the jury had reached a verdict. Soon she was transported back to the courthouse where she met her attorney.

"Buck-up, Nora! We will soon learn what the jury has decided…this battle is not over just yet." David's attempts to cheer Nora were to no avail.

When the Judge was seated, he instructed the bailiff to escort the jurors into the court room. When all were seated, Judge Wolfe turned to the jury and asked, "have you reached a verdict?"

"Yes, Your Honor," the jury foreman answered.

"Very well, the Clerk of Court will take your verdict form," the Judge instructed.

Walking to the jury box, the Clerk accepted the verdict and returned to Judge Wolfe's bench. "Please read the verdict," the Judge instructed the Clerk. "The defendant will please rise."

"Your Honor," the Clerk began, "on the charge for murder of Gregorio Dubliski, the jurors find Nora Dolor guilty of second degree murder. On the charge for the murder of Deputy Clem Sours, the jurors find Nora Dolor guilty of premediated, first degree murder."

Amid the various expressions from the spectators, a loud sob was heard throughout the court room. Nora Dolor, covered her face with trembling hands. She began to uncontrollably weep. Her attorney attempted to console her but her sobbing became only louder.

"We will recess this proceedings until such time that the defendant is able to compose herself," Judge Wolfe rose and exited through the door behind the Judge's bench.

David Grimley attempted to comfort Nora, and, after some time, she was able to speak with a more subdued voice. "Nora, I feel badly about this…we will appeal."

Judge Wolfe soon returned to his bench and spoke to the attorneys and the jurors, "I intend to follow accepted court protocol and, therefore, I will ask the jurors, at the proper time, to impose a sentence on both the second degree verdict and the first degree verdict. I will, at this time, however, poll the jurors and ask if anyone cannot participate in the discussions that could result in a sentence of death for the first degree murder charge. So please stand and explain your position if you intend to oppose the death penalty."

There was uneasiness observed throughout the jury as several shifted in their chairs, however, no one rose to object to their participation. "Very well," the Judge responded to the verbal silence, "…at the proper time we will set the jury to deliberate the sanctions for the two crimes at hand. Court is adjourned and will convene upon my notice."

Again in hand restraints and escorted by two deputies, Nora Dolor began the familiar ride back to the county jail. Once there, she asked to be placed in her cell. Feeling alone, isolated, and abandoned, Nora spent the next several days in a deep depression. She found some hope in what she knew of about the appeal process—it would be many years, she believed, before her case was brought to a final conclusion.

Four days had passed without any word from the court. During those four days her emotions were like a roller-coaster: her spirits up one hour, and then plunging into a deep depressive state the next. "Okay, Nora," a matron alerted her, "you are wanted in court. Something is going on."

Not having time to change into the clothing she had been wearing to court, she appeared in court wearing her much too large orange jump-suit.

"Nora, let me explain what will now take place," her attorney began. "The Judge will now call several witnesses who will speak against the death penalty and several who will speak for such a penalty. Then, the jury will return to the jury room to discuss and decide their decisions about your fate…try to relax…this process could take only hours or several days."

Nora knew none of the witnesses and believed she was a remote spectator, with no recognized interests in the proceedings. By late afternoon all of the witnesses had testified. Their comments basically centered on societal interests: supportive of or undermining social norms. By late evening, Judge Wolfe adjourned court, with admonishments to the jurors to not discuss the proceedings with anyone. Court would convene the next day at 9 A.M.

At the jail Nora gave thought to the witness testimony, wondering if the jurors were influenced in any manner. Nora was surprised that she actually slept well that night. Although not at ease, she was less anxious about the decisions the jurors may render. Again, she allowed herself to believe that perhaps the appeal process would provide respite.

Early the next day jurors had assembled and were nervously pacing in the hall way, waiting for the trial to convene. Judge Wolfe, as he had promised, convened the proceedings promptly at 9 A.M. His first task was to deliver instructions to the jurors, instructions that would guide them as they deliberated sanctions. With no questions from the jury members, the Judge ask the bailiff to escort the jury to the jury room.

It was now a matter of waiting. Nora and David Grimley remained at their table, quietly discussing the elements of the trial, the appeal process, and the possible sanctions that the jury could impose. Nearly five hours had elapsed when the bailiff appeared and summoned the Judge. When the Judge entered the court room and took his place at the bench, he addressed the bailiff and asked for a progress report. The bailiff told the Judge that the jury had reached their decisions. "Bring in the jury," the Judge ordered the bailiff.

The jury members entered the court room, greeted by "ALL RISE," and took their places in the jury box. "Have you reached your decision?" questioned the Judge.

"Yes, Your Honor, we have." The jury foreman answered.

"Please give your verdict to the clerk," the Judge instructed. Then, when the clerk was given the paper with the verdict, the Judge ordered, "the defendant will please stand as the verdict is read."

"Your Honor," the clerk nearly stammered, "the jury has decided that Nora Dolor shall be sentenced to fifty years in prison without parole for the murder of her husband, Gregorio Dubliski; and, Your Honor, the jury recommends the death sentence for the murder of Deputy Clem Sours."

Nora Dolor, with tears streaming down her cheeks, made no sound. She had expected such a sentence and she had no recourse other than to accept the sanctions and rely upon her attorney's abilities to achieve better appeal results.

Judge Wolfe thanked the jury members, and turned to Nora Dolor and David Grimley, "I shall carefully review the jury recommendations; but, I must remind you that I now do not find any reasons to disagree with or reasons to modify the sanctions. Nora Dolor, you shall remain in the custody of the Carbon County Sheriff's department without bail. Court is dismissed. Amid turned heads and whispers, spectators and court officials were surprised that Judge Wolfe had remanded Nora Dolor to the County Sheriff and not to the Department of Corrections. What did Judge Wolfe know that others yet did not know?

"ALL RISE," shouted the bailiff. The Judge, before leaving the court room, instructed the bailiff to bring the jury members into his office.

Before leaving the court room the Judge addressed Dan Lassiter, "Dan, I need for you, Sheriff Overman, and David Grimley to meet with me."

When Dan Lassiter, Sheriff Overman, and David Grimley met with Judge Wolfe they were told: "Gentlemen, we have a problem, perhaps a number of problems. The Department of Corrections has told me that they do not have facilities to hold Nora Dolor for long term confinement. As well, corrections officials are involved in litigation that prevents them from obtaining the proper chemicals necessary to conduct an execution by lethal injection. So, Sheriff Overman, you and Dan Lassiter will need to meet with several legislators who have supported the use of the old prison's gas chamber for state executions. While we have no understanding of how the appeal process will play-out, it may come down to the raw fact that the old gas chamber may be put in operation. Attorney Grimley, you now have untested ground for an interesting appeal. That's it, gentlemen, you have your work cut out for you." Judge Wolfe dismissed the group and sat in his chair looking out of the window in his office—wondering if they were on the proper course for justice.

CHAPTER SIXTEEN

POST TRIAL AND APPEAL PROCESS

Nora Dolor, now a long-term resident of the county jail, settled down for what would become many years of confinement. Her living arrangements had changed considerably. Her cell now contained a television set, a desk, and a continuous supply of books and newspapers. She worked daily at her kitchen assignment, and spent time in the exercise room.

Year after year the appeal process continued. She met frequently with her attorney and was kept informed of the appeal status. She had been well informed of the consequences should her appeals be denied. The thoughts of death in the gas chamber seemed to never subside. Whether watching television, reading, working, or exercising, her thinking would be interrupted by the grim possibility of death. She was haunted by those thoughts.

Although she lived a relatively comfortable life style—she was treated kindly and she enjoyed ample time out of her cell—the years of confinement were beginning to take a toll. Pale, greying hair, and increasing age lines were all reminders of the passing years. Her physical posture was changing now—and she felt lost in the much too large orange jump suit. Where would this all end, she often asked herself?

SHERIFF CHESTER OVERMAN AND DEPUTY LENNY CRAIG

"We need to have a chat," the Sheriff advised Deputy Craig. "Why don't you and Delmar Mentis come over tomorrow afternoon and meet with me?" Deputy Craig agreed to be there per the Sheriff's schedule.

Deputy Craig and Delmar Mentis drove together to Rawlins. They both wondered why the Sheriff wanted them. It was not long before that question was answered.

In the Sheriff's office the conversation began, "Gents, we have some difficult work ahead of us. So far, the appeals for Nora Dolor appear to be going nowhere. To make matters worse, the Department of Corrections advise that they will most likely be unable to obtain the chemicals for a lethal injection. Dan Lassiter and I have been given a green light to prepare for the execution—if it comes to that—to take place at the old gas chamber. The legislators have agreed to make the necessary changes and amendments to the state statute to allow for the gas chamber to once again be used."

The Sheriff paused, picked-up his coffee mug and took a long drink. "I've done a bit of research about executions performed by Sheriff's departments in Wyoming. The last such execution took place on October 26, 1888, in Rawlins, when Benjamin Carter was hanged. That execution was conducted by the Sheriff because the penitentiary, still being built, was unable to conduct the execution. The Sheriff's men performed the execution very well."

"Here we are again. The Department of Corrections is unable to conduct the execution and the job is left to us. This is where you two come in. I need you to go over to the old prison—I have already made the arrangements with the manger of the old place—and evaluate what will be necessary to do to bring the old chamber up to working order. Do what is necessary: employ what services you need, and educate yourselves on the proper use of the chamber. It is now four years into the appeal process and we just don't know when a decision will be made. We may have several more years, however, a decision could crop-up anytime." The Sheriff dismissed the two men and they immediately drove to the old prison.

The day was cold; grey clouds concealed the sun; and wind had begun to whip the snow into drifts. They were greeted by Tonya Mound, the curator of the old prison. With a large key she opened the heavy, iron barred door to the prison. They walked through the old "turnkey's" office and into the cell block A. From there they walked through an iron door and into the cold, windy outdoors. A short walk along a snow-covered side walk led them to the old prison hospital, the building topped by the death house. "Ironic," Deputy Craig commented, "that the building designed to provide medical services and perhaps saves lives has an upper story where people are killed."

They climbed the metal stairway to the door of the death house; opened the iron door; and, as they entered the building, they were soon standing next to the old gas chamber. "Well, here it is," Deputy Craig silently commented. I've seen it before, but it is still a very gruesome structure. Sorta gives you the chills."

"I'm going to leave you two here to do whatever you have to do. Please keep me informed of any and all adjustments and improvements you make. The old prison has a historical designation, and I am obligated to keep records of change and improvements to all parts of the old place." Before leaving Lenny and Delmar, Tonya paused and asked, "…gentlemen, before you begin your inspection, I need to ask you if you have paved your way thus far with the legal requirements necessary to complete the task that lays before you?' She waited for an answer.

"Indeed," Lenny began, "the sheriff has completed the steps necessary to use the old prison here for whatever task the Governor decides. The Governor, I understand, has worked with the state legislature to amend the state statutes so that the gas chamber here can be used…if it comes to that."

Nodding in agreement, Tonya then added: "Please keep in mind that the revenue that we accumulate during tourist season is our life blood. In the event that you should need to use the chamber during tourist season, this old facility and the employees that we have here will be in a very poor situation. I hope that you will pass that fact along."

A glance at Delmar with a frown that revealed that Lenny had not considered the importance of timing for the execution, Lenny cleared his throat and attempted to provide an intelligent answer. "Absolutely, I understand your situation, Tonya, I will certainly convey your concerns to the sheriff, who, I suspect, will then address the subject with the Governor. Hopefully, depending upon the results of the appeals and the time when the appeals are made public, the Governor will be able to convince the state legislature to set an execution date during your off season. We will keep you informed of all activities, especially any dates and times that may be established."

Tonya thanked the two men and departed the death house. As she walked down the stairs of the death house she found herself hoping that the event that may be scheduled for her prison would not disrupt her management concerns. As Tonya left the area Lenny and Delmar set about their duties.

"Better get out your note pad, Delmar. We will need to take down a bunch of notes," Lenny politely instructed.

"To begin," Lenny commented as he opened and entered the door to the chamber, "we will need to hire a plumber to come up here and replace all of the rubber gaskets. The door certainly needs repairs and that exhaust fan up there may have gaskets that need replacing. Also," pointing upward at the exhaust fan, "we need to have an electrician examine the fan to make certain it is operating properly. These old windows also may need to be replaced—better have a glazier come up and inspect them. These ports around the bottom of the chamber need to be inspected...I suspect that there are rubber gaskets in these ports that probably need to be replaced."

Walking to the metal chair in the center of the floor, Lenny tested the metal rod that would drop the cyanide "pills" into a pan filled with sulfuric acid. "This all seems to work properly."

The two men left the interior of the chamber and walked to the rear and then around the chamber. Lenny summed-up their inspection, "We will need to have this area cleaned-up---pretty dirty. Also, it may be a good idea to paint the exterior of the chamber with similar aluminum paint. We have to remember that there will be ten witnesses who will attend the execution. Better have the cell block that serves the death house also cleaned. We may need to use it as waiting areas for people who will assist with the execution."

"Oh, yes, almost forgot this item," Lenny said as he walked to the old telephone loosely attached to the wall, "...we need to have the telephone people come up and give us a working telephone. Before the execution can proceed a call to the Governor for his permission to begin is necessary. So, the phone is pretty important."

"It's getting dark up here, so we better call it a day. And, that reminds me, that we will need electricity up here. So, the electric company needs to get in on this," Lenny concluded.

Colder now, as they walked from the death house back to the "turnkey's" office where they met Tonya. They returned the key to the death house and thanked her for allowing them to inspect the old chamber. Before leaving they informed her of the work necessary to bring the old chamber up to a safe level of operation.

At the Sheriff's department Deputy Craig and Delmar Mentis informed the Sheriff of their inspection and the work that would be necessary before the old chamber could be used. The Sheriff gave his full attention as they explained the repairs that were necessary. When asked if jail inmates could be used to clean and paint, the Sheriff gave his approval. "Okay, gents, I want you both to do some research on the procedures necessary to conduct a fail-safe, error-free execution. The last time the old chamber was used was December 10, 1965, when Andrew Pixley was executed. Go over to the archives. There should be a pretty detailed report in some of the old Board of Charities and Reform files. Also, there should be a number of old news paper articles that may get you some additional information." With that the Sheriff told them that he was now in almost daily contact with state legislators who wanted progress reports and, as well, who advised him that, should the execution be conducted, they expected neither complications nor errors.

Deputy Craig and Delmar Mentis, before leaving Rawlins for their return to their homes, made arrangements for their trip to Cheyenne and the archives. With no decisions that yet had been handed down regarding the appeals, they were under neither pressure to complete the research ordered by the Sheriff nor to upgrade the old chamber.

NORA DOLOR CONTINUES TO WAIT

"It does not look good, Nora," David Grimley informed her. "...the information that I have received suggests that all lower courts have rejected the appeal pleadings. Any National groups opposing the death penalty have now stepped aside, giving attention to other matters. We now rely upon the United States Supreme court and the Wyoming Supreme court. You best prepare yourself, Nora, as a decision could be made at any time. Forget not, Nora, the appeals process now enters the eighth year. A decision could be forthcoming at any time."

Nora stared blankly at the floor. At what point should I begin to panic? Should she attempt to remain confident that her life would be spared by a decision to over-turn the death sentence?

Her anxiety was not lessened by visits from the Department of Corrections officials who seemed more interested in "final affairs" than in monitoring her status at the jail. At one point she thought that she could delay all proceedings by contesting the fact that she had been remanded to the Sheriff's department rather than the Department of Corrections. Her attorney advised her that any such loop-holes had been resolved by the actions taken by the state legislature and the amendment of laws that gave the Sheriff's department full authority in the matter.

Nora Dolor, eight years older now, was not bearing the passage of time well. Her hair was now nearly grey; worry and age lines let those around her to understand that she was under great stress; and her interest in daily activities had been replaced by withdrawal. She could only wait.

#3 hospital and DEATH house

#4 Stairway to Death House

#6 metal chair in Th Gas Chamber

#5 Gas Chamber Door

THE OLD GAS CHAMBER

Work was rapidly being completed to correct issues with the old chamber. A plumber, an electrician, a glazier, and cleaning crews had nearly completed their repairs. Deputy Craig and Delmar Mentis had written policies and procedures that explained the duties of each person who would participate in the execution. Training sessions, being conducted, emphasized each task necessary to properly complete the execution. Each person designated to assist with the execution knew exactly how to perform their assigned tasks. When all was considered ready to "give life" to the old chamber, the chamber was tested to ensure that it was air-tight and safe to use. A smoke-bomb was ignited in the chamber to test rubber gaskets and new windows. A representative of the Wyoming Environmental Protection agency was present to monitor the test. The old chamber was considered to be air-tight and safe to employ.

THE TIME HAD ARRIVED

Sheriff Overman summoned Deputy Craig with the news. "Well, ten years now, and I was just informed that the execution is to be conducted on January 22, 1992. The Governor called me and the Attorney General's office just got off the phone. They asked me if we were ready. Lenny, are we ready?"

"Yes, Sir," Lenny answered, "Everything is in order. The execution team is well trained—we will do one more walk-through. The chamber has undergone extensive repairs—and it has been successfully tested. I have all of the chemicals that we will need stored in a safe and secure location." Remembering his conversation with Tonya Mound, Lenny spoke, almost as if he was assuring himself of a promise made, "the date for the execution is perfect as that date will not interfere with the Old Prison's tourist season."

NORA DOLOR

David Grimley looked forward to his meeting with Nora with nearly dreaded anticipation. When he arrived at the jail, Nora was at her work assignment in the kitchen. A matron escorted her to the room where her attorney waited. She entered the room; her breathing became labored; she almost knew the reason that her attorney had visited.

"Nora," David nearly mumbled, "...the news is bad, extremely very bad. All court levels have now found no merit in the appeals that have been filed. An execution date has been scheduled for January 22, 1992. I will file a brief with the Governor and the Supreme court, but probably, to no avail. I just do not know what more I can do for you."

Nora began to sob—her entire body violently trembled. Her tears were copious. "I knew it was coming. I just tried to hold on to some hope," she managed to say through her sobbing. "I guess I just have to now try to meet my end with some dignity."

"Can I do anything for you, Nora?" David asked. "Would you like to meet with a religious counselor? I can make such arrangements."

"No," Nora despondently answered. "I have made my way through life relying on few others. I will continue to do that now. I have no family members and no close friends, so I am on my own. I will do the best with what is left in me. I do regret what I have done, but I can't change that now."

"Nora, this is difficult to discuss, but I am obligated to ask you what arrangements you want made following the execution?" David asked in a low voice.

"Do whatever is necessary—cremation or burial—it will no longer be of concern for me," She answered.

Nora was left with her thoughts and that which remained of her life.

DELMAR MENTIS

Rhonda was standing nearby when Delmar received word of the scheduled execution. She had remained quiet during the time that he and Deputy Craig had trained for the execution. Now, nearly at the eve of the execution, she turned to Delmar and quietly whispered, "I knew that this would not end well." Rhonda, just before Delmar walked from the kitchen to the door of their cabin, placed her arms around Delmar and gave him a kiss on his cheek.

DEPUTY LENNY CRAIG

He had painstakingly completed the investigation, and he had been successful as a participant in the proceedings that had found Nora Dolor guilty of murder. "I know that this must bother you, Lenny," his wife

Kathy consoled. "You are just doing your job. I will be here to assist you in every way." She placed her arms around Lenny and laid her head on his shoulder.

SHERIFF CHESTER OVERMAN

The time had arrived. He had been ordered to begin the execution promptly at midnight on January 22, 1992. Assembled in his office late that evening he gave final instructions to Deputy Craig and Delmar Mentis. "So we don't botch this up with legal issues, I will deputize Delmar. That way he can assist in any official capacity. I will wait here in my office to handle any phone calls. I will have a male deputy and two jail matrons escort Nora Dolor to the old prison. Let's not take her over there too early. I'll give you a jingle when she is on her way. Okay, that's about it. Are all of your team members ready and assembled? How about the witnesses?"

"Everything is ready, Sheriff. Team members are ready, and witnesses will be picked-up at their homes or businesses so that way we will all arrive at the same time. I have a police officer who will tend to and monitor the witnesses. We are set to go, Sheriff," Lenny stated confidently.

"Good luck, men. Remember that you are just doing your sworn duty.

PREPARATIONS

Deputy Craig and Delmar Mentis drove to the old prison and waited there for all of the team members to arrive. The night was dark; wind blew, rattling old windows and doors; and as they walked through cell block A, eerie sounds made by the wind slamming the exterior wall seemed to welcome intruders with a grave warning. Deputy Craig left two police officers at the front door to assist team members and to ward-off uninvited guests.

It was now 10:45 P.M. and time for Nora Dolor to arrive. Once there, accompanied by the matrons and the male deputy, she also walked the path to the death house. A path had been shoveled free of snow, but the wind had created drifts along the way. Nora attempted to step around the drifts but her jail slippers soon filled with the cold snow. One of the matrons told Lenny that they had attempted to calm Nora, but they probably had not well anticipated her reaction when they told her how the execution would unfold. She became somewhat hysterical, the matron admitted. Now, as she reached the death house she was silent and seemed emotionally calm. She stood at the bottom of the metal stairs leading to the death house. With her hands restrained she was unable to grasp the metal railing and her efforts to climb the stairs limited her to a single step at a time. One matron stepped in front of Nora while the second matron supported her from behind. Assisted by the matrons they finally reached the door to the death house. Upon entering the death house, she immediately caught a glimpse of the chamber...it was positioned in a small room immediately to her left. Had she been briefed on the history of the old prison, she would have noticed the opening in the wall, directly in front of her, that led to the old hanging chamber. Had she given a more careful glance, she would have seen the metal ring on the ceiling, just above where the trap door had been positioned—the metal ring where the hangman's ropes had been secured. Before she was able to stop and more closely examine the chamber, she was escorted down a hall way to her right to a holding cell that was located to the south of the room where the chamber was located. There she remained with the two matrons who attempted to sooth her with light conversation.

As the witnesses climbed the long stairway to the death house, they tightened coats and scarves in an attempt to ward-off the cold—most thought that it was not the cold, but rather chills of nervousness they were attempting to allay. The witnesses, escorted by a police officer, were guided to the rear of the chamber where they met Dr. Purdy who stood with a stethoscope connected by a plastic tube running through a very small hole in the chamber wall...directly behind the metal chair. This plastic tube, connected to a heart monitor, would soon be placed on Nora Dolor's heart area.

All was ready. Deputy Craig looked quickly at his watch. It was now 11:50 P.M. He asked all present for their silence as he telephoned first Sheriff Overman and then the Governor. Both individuals gave their approval for the execution to begin at 12 P.M.

RAWLINS DAILY NEWS...JANUARY 22, 1990

This reporter was selected to witness and report upon the execution of Nora Dolor, an aging woman who has been incarcerated in the county jail for the past ten years. This woman is accused of and was sentenced for the death of her husband and for the murder of Deputy Clem Sours.

Before beginning my assignment, I thought it best to arm myself with a variety of facts about the executions that have taken place at the old prison. Perhaps my efforts only served to heighten my trepidation about actually witnessing an execution. Nevertheless, this is what I learned: Since statehood, July 10, 1890, there have been a total of eighteen executions conducted by the state of Wyoming. The first four executions were conducted by County Sheriffs. I found that two of the hangings took place in Cheyenne; one took place in Lander; and one in Rawlins. After 1903, fourteen of the eighteen executions were performed at the Wyoming State Penitentiary. Nine of the executions were by hanging and five by lethal gas. Interesting, I thought, was that one of the men executed at the old prison was a Federal prisoner. There I was, about to be a witness to another execution at the old prison, equipped with facts—that I had to admit later—would serve me of no use.

While there has been comments from both those who oppose the execution and from those who favored the reasons for the execution, this reporter will remain neutral and merely explain the events that occurred throughout the execution. A telephone call to the Governor's office, asking if the Governor may, at the last minute, commute the death sentence, was curtly answered: "At this time the Governor has no plans to commute the sentence." It should be remembered that the old gas chamber has not been used since December 10,1965; however, Sheriff Overman claims that the chamber has been renovated and is safe for the execution.

Assembled with ten witnesses, I was able to see very well the interior of the chamber through the window where I was standing. The witnesses, standing next to me, included a police man, David Grimley, the condemned woman's attorney, two assistants from the Coroner's office, a member of the clergy, four members at-large from the community, and a representative of the Department of Corrections. Deputy Craig left the chamber momentarily and soon returned with Deputy Delmar Mentis:

both men entered the chamber carrying several containers. Later I was informed that one container consisted of the sulfuric-acid that was placed in a plastic pan located beneath the metal chair that sat in the center of the room. In another container was the anhydrous-ammonia "charges" that were placed in the four ports located at several places on the lower walls of the chamber. This chemical, I was told, would be injected into the chamber, once the condemned woman was declared dead, as a means to neutralize the cyanide fumes. Finally, a member of the fire department, fully suited with proper clothing and wearing a breathing apparatus, entered the chamber carrying a cheese cloth-appearing sack which was later explained to me as the container filled with the cyanide pellets. This sack was attached to a metal bar located beneath the chair. Witness were now shifting nervously as each knew that the hour had nearly arrived.

Then I witnessed the condemned woman. She appeared very haggard, but moving quickly when instructed to do so. She was escorted into the chamber, rather clumsily I might add, by the matrons. The door to the chamber is an oval, maritime-type door. The lower portion of the door is about six inches above the floor, causing anyone who enters to step over the raised opening. One matron entered first, turning with arms extending to assist the condemned woman. As she was helping the woman to enter the chamber, the woman slightly stumbled, nearly falling. Both matrons then supported the woman and finally brought her safely into the chamber. The condemned woman was wearing a hospital-type gown, secured with straps at the back.

The matrons led her to the metal chair, which the defendant seemed to eye disapprovingly. One matron assisted the woman to sit in the chair with her arms resting on the metal arms of the chair. The second matron secured her arms to the arms of the chair with available restraints. Then, this same matron knelt down and secured the defendant's legs with restraining straps. Finally, a leather strap was placed around the condemned woman's chest. While the woman was being secured to the metal chair, she seemed to be trying to speak to the matrons. The matrons merely patted her shoulders and continued their work. Deputy Craig then entered the chamber, stood before Nora Dolor and read the order for execution to her. Craig asked the woman if she understood the order. She nodded her head. Then, before leaving the chamber, the matrons whispered something to the

woman—possibly telling her to breath deeply, not to hold her breath—
then they both left the chamber.

Dr. Purdy entered the chamber once the matrons had left. He walked
to the woman sitting in the chair and placed a heart monitoring device
of some type on her left upper chest area. Dr. Purdy left the chamber and
returned to his place at the outside, rear of the chamber.

As various officials entered and exited the chamber, the condemned
woman watched with mounting alarm as the various tasks were completed.
Often her eyes would rest on the windows, eyes clearly filled with fear and
even terror.

Deputy Craig was seen placing a padlock on the door—as a measure
to prevent anyone from trying to enter the chamber to stop the execution.
Immediately, Deputy Craig was seen removing a latching pin from the
metal arm that controlled the movement of the metal rod that held the
cyanide pellets. He then pulled the metal arm forward causing the cyanide
pellets to slowly enter the pan of liquid sitting beneath the condemned
woman. Within seconds a slight mist engulfed Nora Dolor. She was seen
breathing deeply, with barely no observable struggle. At one point her body
seemed to convulse with a slight struggle against her restraints. Within
five minutes, Dr. Purdy announced that there was no longer a heart-beat.
Nora Dolor had now paid the full price for her crimes.

Deputy Craig was then observed speaking with the member of the
fire department, preparing him for the next task to be completed. The
witnesses around me were silent…no one expressed their thoughts of what
they had just witnessed. As the witnesses and I watched the proceedings we
saw the chamber being flooded with the anhydrous-ammonia, the solution
that neutralized the cyanide fumes. The interior of the chamber was now
cloudy and restricting sight into the chamber. Nora Dolor sat slumped in
the chair seeming to patiently wait while the work of the team members
was being conducted. Deputy Craig then activated the exhaust fan and
soon the chamber was clear of any chemicals.

The member of the fire department entered the chamber, walked to
Nora Dolor, roughly ruffled her hair and forcefully pumped her chest.
This, I was later told, was to release any cyanide fumes that may linger in
her hair and any fumes that would remain in her lungs. Dr. Purdy entered
the chamber and removed the heart monitoring device. He then directed

two of his assistants to place Nora Dolor's body in a black bag and remove her from the chamber. Removing her body became a most difficult task. First, exiting through the oval door was not without much effort to avoid dropping the body. Then, as the assistants began their decent of the stairways, additional help from the police and fire department became necessary. Finally, the body was placed in the Coroner's van that had been backed into the space in front of the old hospital. Her body was then transported to the coroner's office.

The task had been completed. Deputy Craig was seen talking on the telephone, probably telling either the Sheriff or the Governor that the execution was successfully completed. We, the public, can only wonder now if Deputy Clem Sours rests more peacefully.

EPILOGUE

Deputy Lenny Craig, the coyote, stood among the witnesses watching the removal of Nora Dolor's body. His face, somber and ashen, reflected not the satisfaction he had once witnessed while pursuing his prey. Now, inner thoughts about his conquest were creating confusion. His patience as the hunter had brought the prey to what he believed to be a justifiable end. He had the rest of his life to consider that conclusion.

The magpie, Delmar Mentis, stood at the top of the metal stairway, watching the cumbersome removal of Nora Dolor's body. His thoughts returned to his wife, Rhonda, when she had offered to him the warning that: "This will not end well."

MAGPIE AND COYOE

The magpie thought: "I will sit on a horn and scream. I cannot eat until the pain is over, the flesh quits moving, and the smell is dead." Anonymous Native American…Wyoming State Prison

"Is it better to have laws and obey…or to hunt and kill?" Piggy … LORD OF THE FLIES (William Golding)

"One who is injured ought not to return the injury, for on no account can it be right to do an injustice; and it is not right to return an injury, or to do evil to any man, however much we have suffered from him." SOCRATES

Only those with the responsibility to open and close a grave attended the burial of Irana Dubliski. She had been given a place among others who had either died at the hands of the executioner or who, in other ways, had met their end in the old prison.

END

Printed in the United States
By Bookmasters